Geena and Amanda,
you are my greatest inspiration.

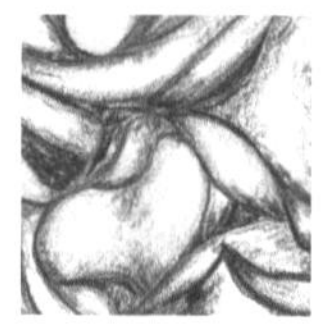

Cecelia's Garden, Nurturing Creative Thinking

www.joannsondy.com

Published by:
Creative Aces Publishing
Chicago, IL 60657

Cover art:
© 2019 Joann B. Sondy, "Gardenia",
soft pastel on Strathmore® pastel paper 11″ x 14″

Interior art/illustrations:
© 2019 Joann B. Sondy

ISBN: 978-0-984-8950-7-6

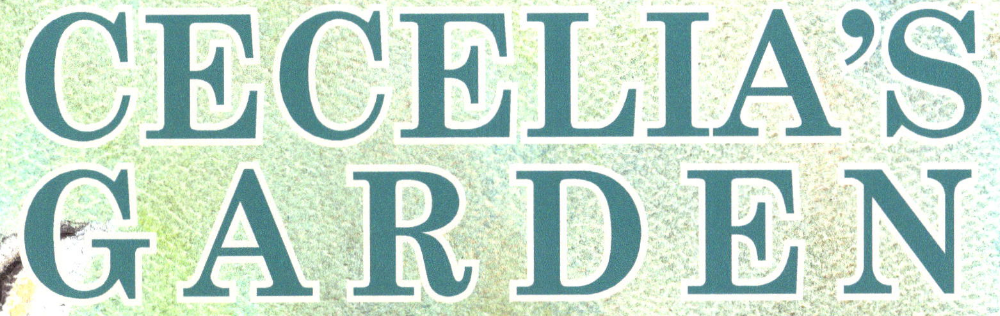

NURTURING CREATIVE THINKING

JOANN B. SONDY
AUTHOR & ILLUSTRATOR

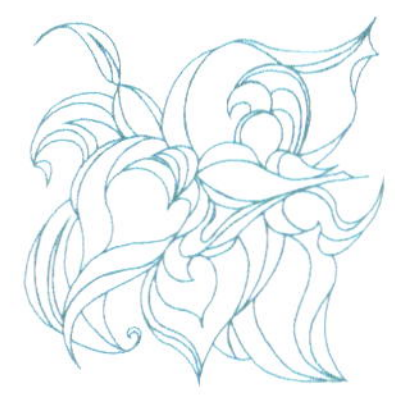

CONTENTS

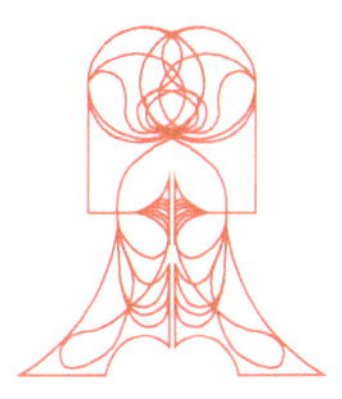

INTRODUCTION

How does one sustain a decades-long creative career? The answer eluded me as I approached a career crisis. Insight came to me, out of nowhere, in the form of a memory about my mother Cecelia. My unexpected inspiration was triggered by the thought of her infectious laugh and her love for flowers. They became a formula, more like a recipe, for creative success.

I grew up at a time when 'housewife' was a common job description. Cecelia Allen was Roy Allen's wife. She also was my mother. At times it seemed like she was my oldest sister. Cecelia Allen was always my mentor. Even though she never described herself as a "teacher", teaching turned out to be one her strongest assets.

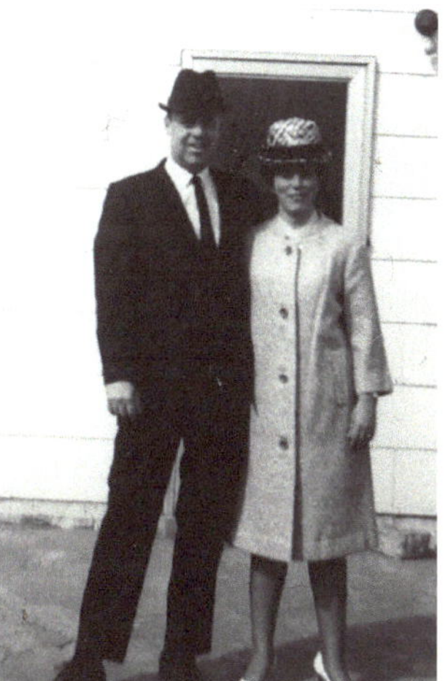

Cecelia and Roy (Mom and Dad) encouraged their children work with their hands:

Sewing, knitting, crocheting and embroidery;
Home decor, gardening, cooking, and baking;
Ceramics, sculpture, watercolor and oil painting;
Car restoration and small engine repair; and
Assembling model cars and woodcraft.

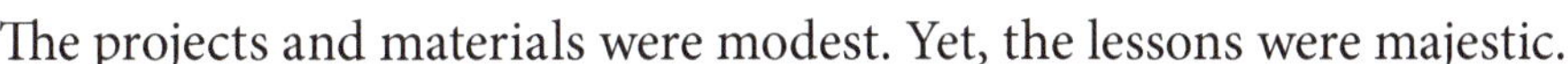

The projects and materials were modest. Yet, the lessons were majestic.

My creative thinking and problem solving skills were embedded at an early age; instilled through the use of construction paper, crayons and glue.

As a parent, I knew that developing my children's creative thinking skills were paramount. Adapting my mother's techniques into my own parenting experience inspired me to spur their creativity. That old reliable bucket of crayons and newsprint spread out on the kitchen table worked for my children just like it worked for me. After school and rainy days were times to encourage my kids to doodle, draw. and giggle, as they sipped Kool-Aid and munched BP&J sandwiches.

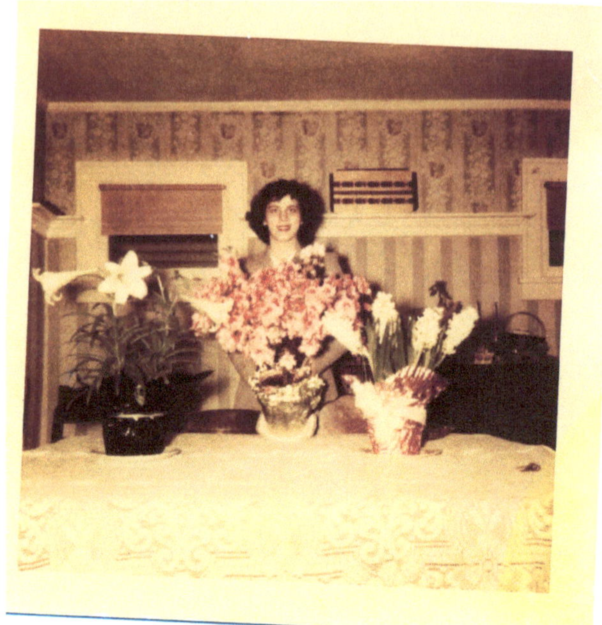

I am a life-long advocate of arts in school. My artistic education is rooted in those public school classes, teachers and programs. The suburban school district where I grew up was flush with funding. Those funds enabled it to offer robust curriculums that included art and music. I sought many opportunities, including 'special' permission from the high school principal to enroll in the boys-only drafting class. It was a time when girls were not thought to have youthful curiosity. Girls weren't considered when it came to exploring new ideas or experimenting with materials. Those things were reserved for boys.

My creativity and creative thinking developed early. It evolved into a driving passion, that still continues define me decades later.

Cecelia's Garden is a collection of stories about an unknowingly creative mentor and 'creative thinking' that can be applied to every day life.

Creativity is as important as literacy and numeracy, and I actually think people understand that creativity is important– they just don't understand what it is.

Sir Ken Robinson

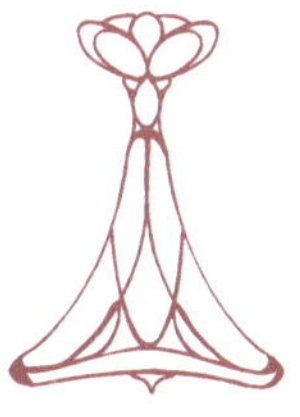

PERFUME TRUMPET

Joann stood there, on the threshold, eyes glancing about the room. Bed, dresser, trunk, drawing table, double closet...whispering to herself, "*my own room!*"

Her new bedroom was once the original master bedroom of the classic three-bedroom suburban ranch she called home. It had been Roy and Cecelia's master suite. After a new addition had been completed, their new boudoir was now on the second floor,. Little brother, Brian's room was moved upstairs, too. *Thank goodness.* Two older sisters were gone, married and setting up their own houses with their new husbands.

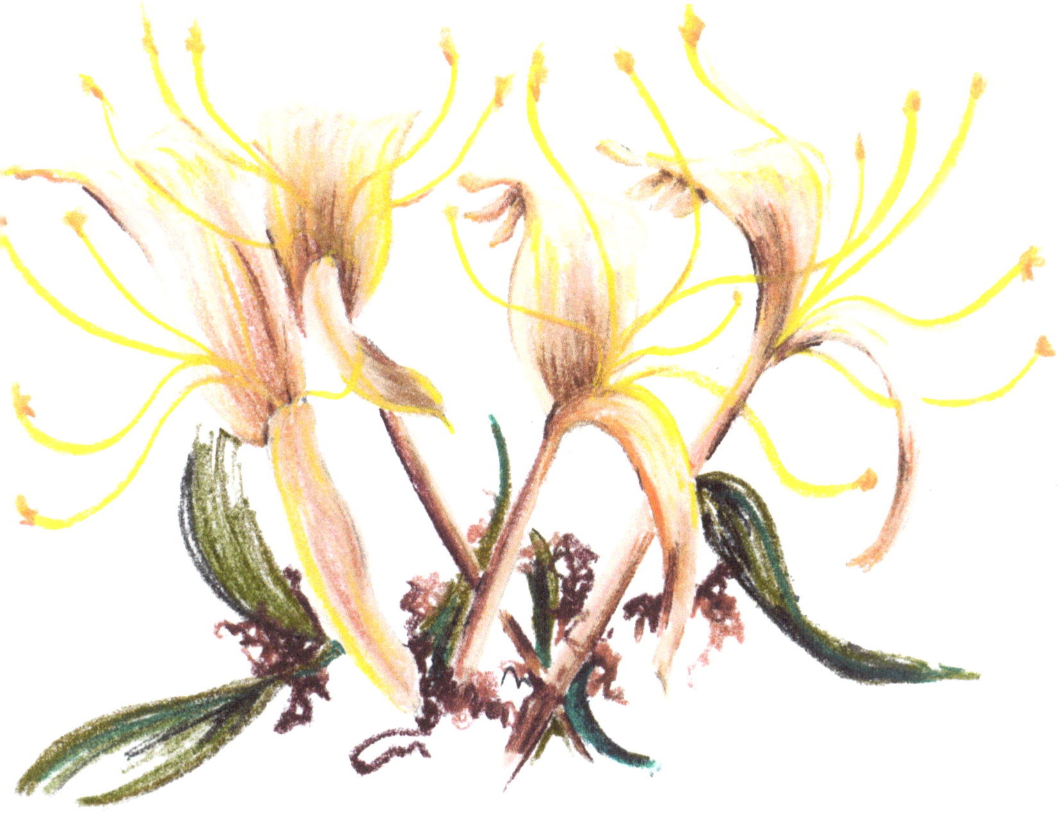

Joann had shared a bedroom with one of her older sisters until she was a teenager. Finally, she had a room to call her own.

That moment of joy was accompanied by the gentle breezes of fresh air floating into the room through the open window. The staleness of the winter drifted away as the perfume from the honeysuckle outside the window wafted in. The fragrance was sweet and welcoming. It was a marvelous aroma that was a signal from Cecelia's garden: Spring had arrived.

Ready for a night's work, Joann perched herself on the stool in front of her drawing and painting table. She was ready for an evening of work. The honeysuckle perfume augmented her level of concentration and boosted her acute attention to the details of the painting project at hand.

Why was the honeysuckle placed outside our home's original master bedroom? Cecilia had to have been consciously aware of its intoxicating aroma. Was she creating a romantic atmosphere behind closed doors? [*Wink, Wink*]

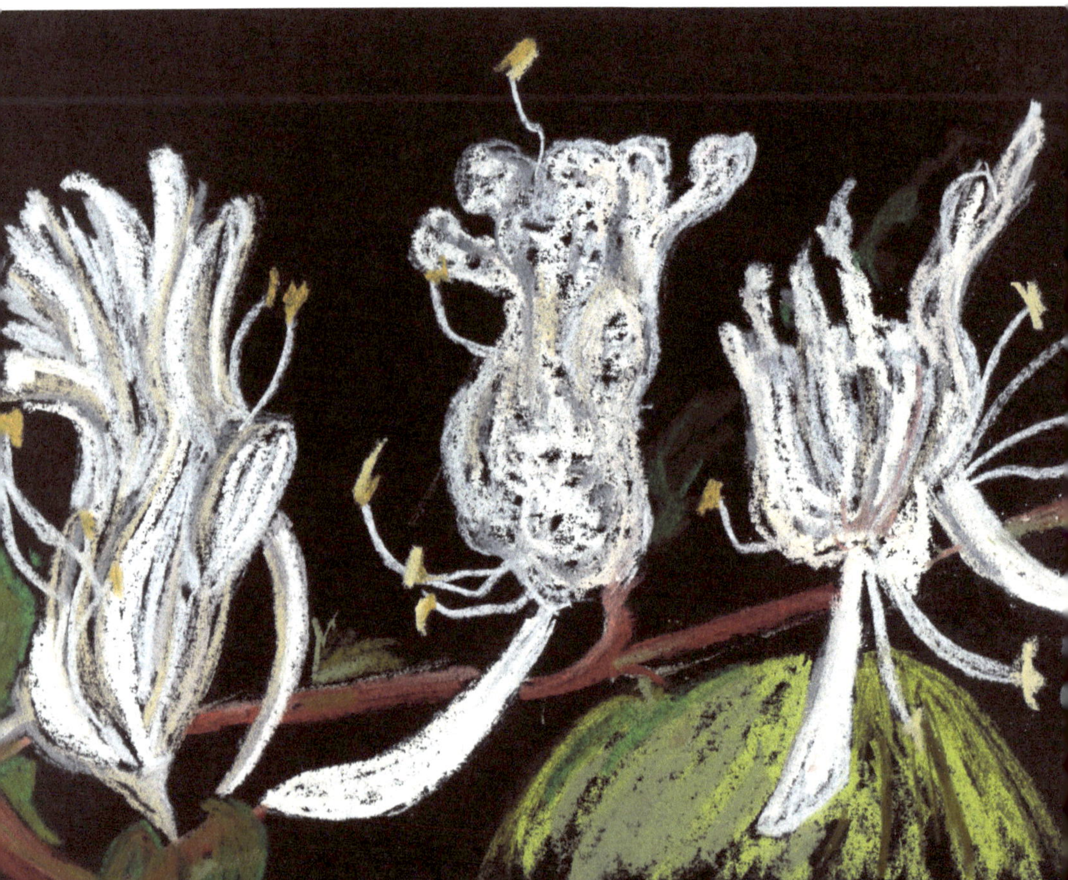

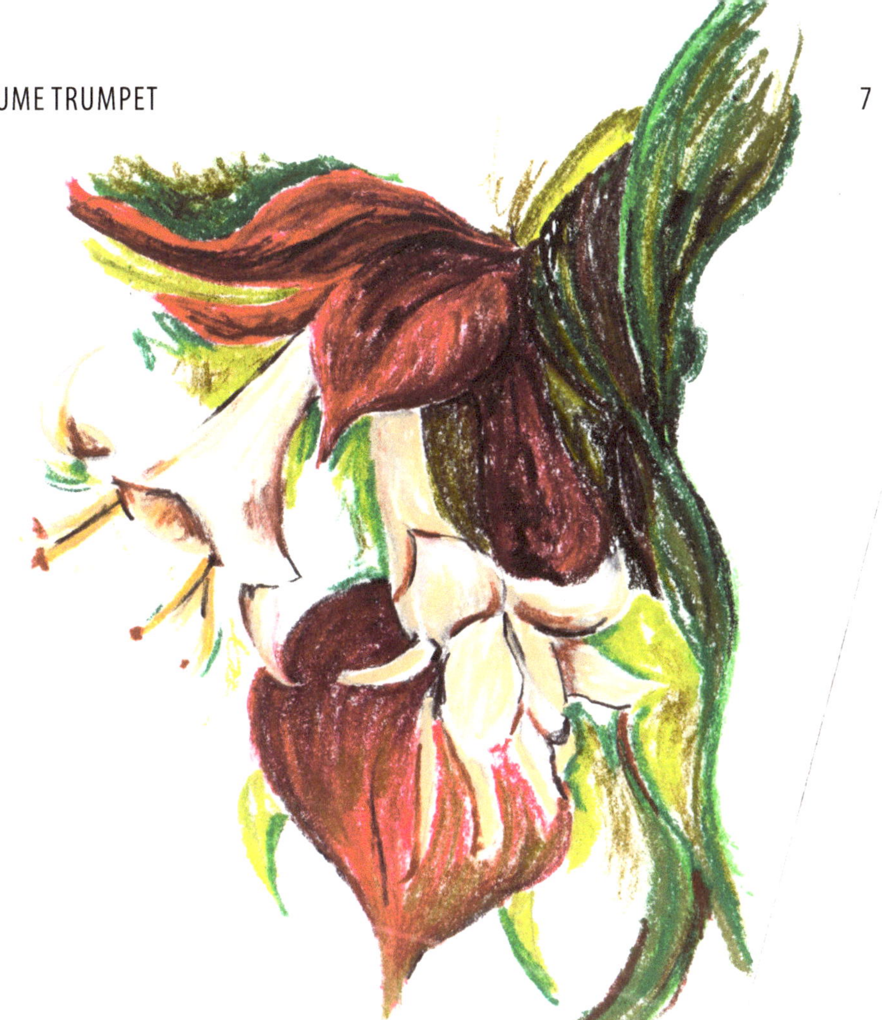

During the Victorian Era, it was believed that honeysuckle could ward off witches and evil spirits.

This southern corner of the garden was bathed in both morning and afternoon sun. It was a perfect location for a honeysuckle plant to mature. The willowy flexible vines were filled with small green leaves. This beautiful blossoming plant made a lush backdrop for the other flowering plants in the garden.

As diligent gardeners, Roy and Cecelia knew that the plant would quickly grow out-of-control without proper supervision. They did their best to trim, manage and control the growth of their cherished honeysuckle.

Cecelia's Creative Counsel:

Subtle.

Superstition.

Unexpected.

The influences of sensory elements, like scent, can be very powerful.

No one has yet developed "smell-o-vision". It will come, one day.

Are you letting your senses be ignited?

- Taste
- Vision
- Touch
- Sound
- Smell

Sensory play contributes to learning and creativity.

Honeysuckle blossoms have a fascinating and complex shape. Their flowers can be orange, red, white or, most commonly, yellow. The early buds were white and tubular shaped. Cecelia's honeysuckle blooms matured to warm rich yellow. The exploding petals grew into the shape of miniature trumpets.

Delicate flowers are an invitation for the pollen seekers. Butterflies and bees often visited our yard. They flittered around the blossoms, playfully dancing from flower to flower. Their job, collecting and transferring the pollen from one plant to the next, was a labor they performed with effortless energy

Our garden was an amazing place of exploration. It was never lacking interesting creatures, colorful birds, butterflies, bees, fireflies, grasshoppers, and crickets made our garden their home. There was no need for store-bought bird feeders. Our homemade projects were placed around the yard and attracted nature's best to Cecelia's garden.

When summer came to a close, Roy would cut back the honeysuckle bush to its main branches. He trimmed a few branches back to the maintain structure so they wouldn't interfere with the nearby roses and peonies. The debris was tossed onto the compost pile in the back corner of the yard.

Dormant for the winter, the honeysuckle rested in anticipation for the release of its sweet citrus perfume next spring.

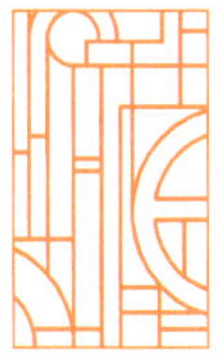

BABY CARROTS

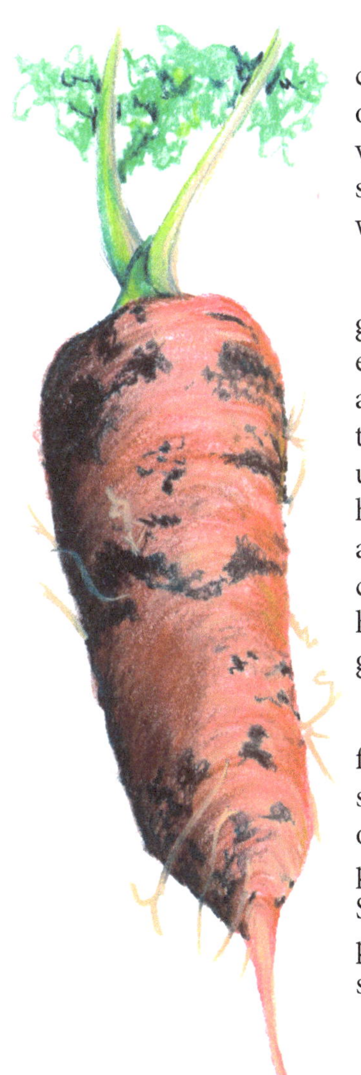

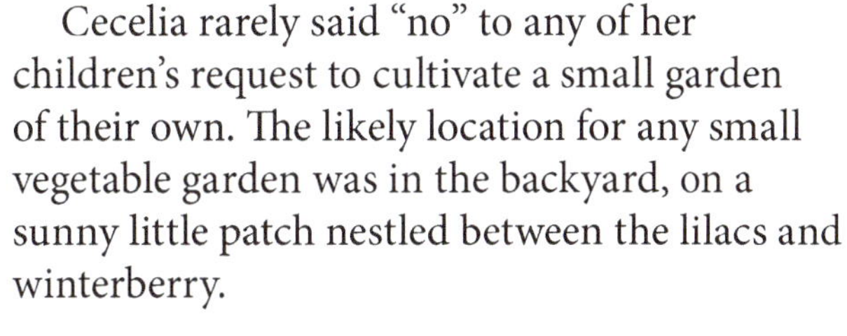

Cecelia rarely said "no" to any of her children's request to cultivate a small garden of their own. The likely location for any small vegetable garden was in the backyard, on a sunny little patch nestled between the lilacs and winterberry.

Cecelia was a wonderful coach. She offered guidance as well as instruction. Cecelia explained all of the steps involved in cultivating a vegetable garden. First, we gathered the tools to prepare our garden. We needed to clear unwanted weeds and debris that would have hampered our garden's growth. A rake and a shovel were used to loosen the soil and add compost enriching the soil. Detailed preparation had to be completed before any plants could be given a new home.

We didn't simply drop seeds directly into the freshly prepared soil. Germinating vegetable seeds indoors was our favored option. The old trick of layering seeds between moistened paper towels was done weeks in advance inside. Sometimes we would also plant seeds in little peat pots and place them on the windowsill until sprouts emerged.

Seed packets were inexpensive and readily available. They were almost always on display at our local grocery store or garden center. Even the farmer's market sold seed packets. The three-by-four inch illustrated envelopes of vegetables and flowers were available for mere pennies.

Cecilia was all too familiar with children's commitment levels. She limited choices by recommending carrots, radishes and green onions. Cecelia knew that any young gardener could reap the bounty of these vegetables without tremendous effort or special attention.

For a child, the process of germinating seeds is a slow and boring. There is so little progress in the early stages. Youngsters have limited attention spans. A few minutes each day for watering and observation, measuring the sprouts; and accounting for seeds not sprouted. Learning to be patient and observation in childhood would become valuable lessons later on in life.

The tricky part was transporting the sprouts from the windowsill to the prepared garden in the backyard. It was about twenty yards from the back door to our little garden patch. Little hands, balancing an important load while being careful with each step, made the short walk seem more like a mile.

The little brown peat pots were kept along side folded wet paper towel containing freshly germinated sprouts on a cookie sheet for their journey. A firm grip on the cookie sheet, along with Mom's guiding hand, steadied the tender shoots as they bounced across the yard.

After a slow painstaking walk to our destination, we carefully placed the cookie sheet on the grass in front of our garden patch. We dug straight shallow ditches with the hand trowel and placed the seedlings-in-peat-pots in the dirt first. The garden was divided into three sections; one for the carrots, another for radishes and the last section for green onions.

Finally, we replaced the soil we had dug out around the peat pots and planted the paper towel sprouts; gently patting the soil firmly over them. "*Careful, you don't want it buried too deep*," Cecelia advised.

The green nylon hose was dragged out from its reel under the kitchen window on the sole condition, that it would be returned to its proper place when we were finished with it. Mom turned on the spigot, just enough to create a soft trickle of water.

"*We'll check on your garden tomorrow, let them be*," she said.

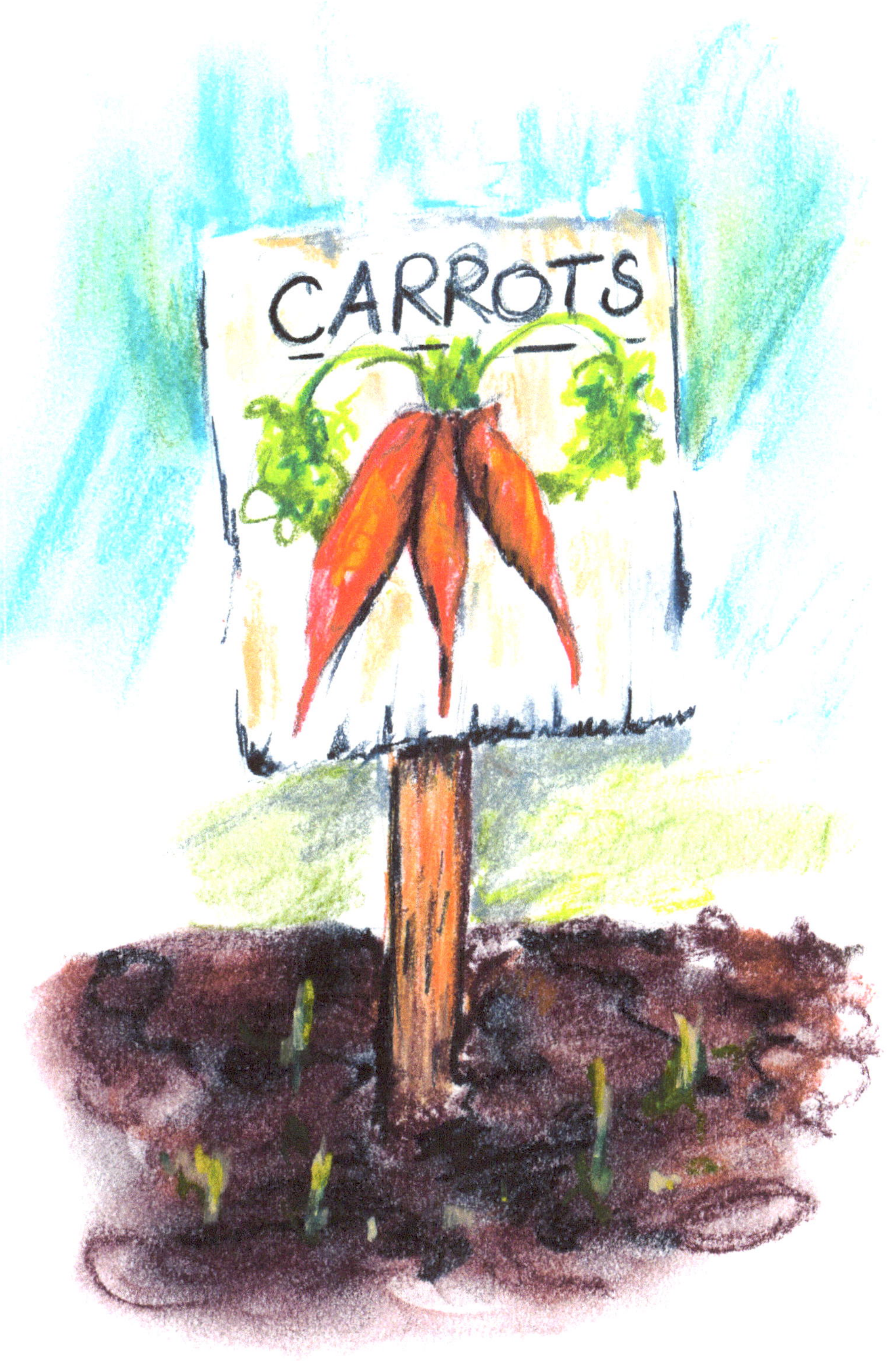
CARROTS

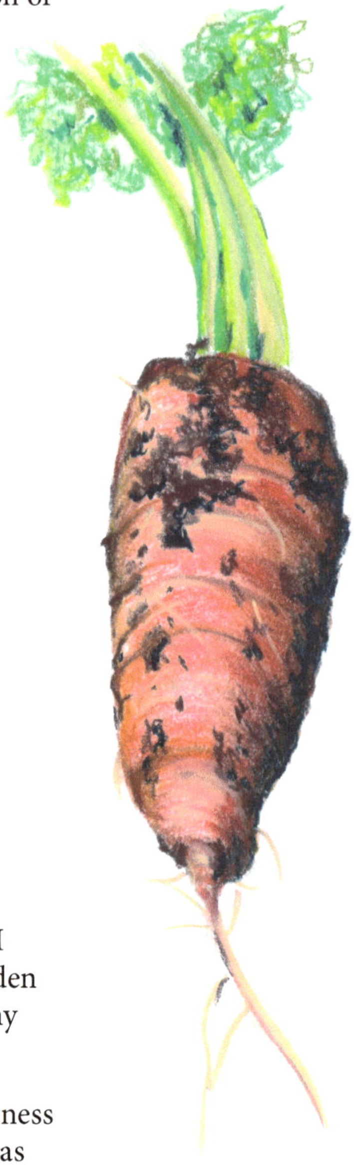

Back in the kitchen, we retrieved Popsicle sticks from the craft cabinet to make markers for each section of the garden we had just planted. Instead of cutting the picture from the seed packet, we made small drawings of carrots, radishes and green onions. Then we cut and pasted our artwork onto one end of the stick leaving enough of the wooden Popsicle stick exposed to plant into the soil. I remember running out to the freshly planted garden, inserting the little signs into the dirt. Their placement wasn't always precise, and, it didn't matter if the sprouts were misidentified.

Keeping the dog and my little redheaded brother, Brian, away from the veggie garden was paramount! I was determined to have homegrown carrots, radishes, and green onions. Another sibling battle had begun.

Cool spring days with rain, turned to warm summer days. The plants grew and grew. Their green tops got bigger and bigger. Surely, there were vegetables under the dirt. I checked on the progress of the vegetable garden after school and would have more time for my little garden once summer vacation started.

"*Can we see?*" Brian and I shared an eagerness to harvest the vegetables. Our anticipation was palpable and thrilling. It was almost as exciting as hearing the Good Humor truck come down the block on a hot summer afternoon.

The fuzzy green tops of the carrots were several inches tall. Leafy green radishes tops fought in silent competition for sunlight. Green onions, were standing tall with their slender straw-like stalks stretched skyward with eager growth. *"Another few weeks, then they'll be ready to pull,"* Cecelia said, tempering our enthusiasm.

The wait was excruciating. I couldn't hold back another day. Down on my knees, I reached out, grabbed one of the dark green, curly tops of a carrots and I pulled up a handful of fresh CARROT.

Little Joann studied the tapered orange root she held in the palm of her hand. It had black dirt clinging to it, with a bit more lose dirt spilling back into the garden. Tightly holding her prized carrot, Joann turned and ran into the house. The carrot root with flecks of dirt was her gold medal. She proudly presented it to her Mom.

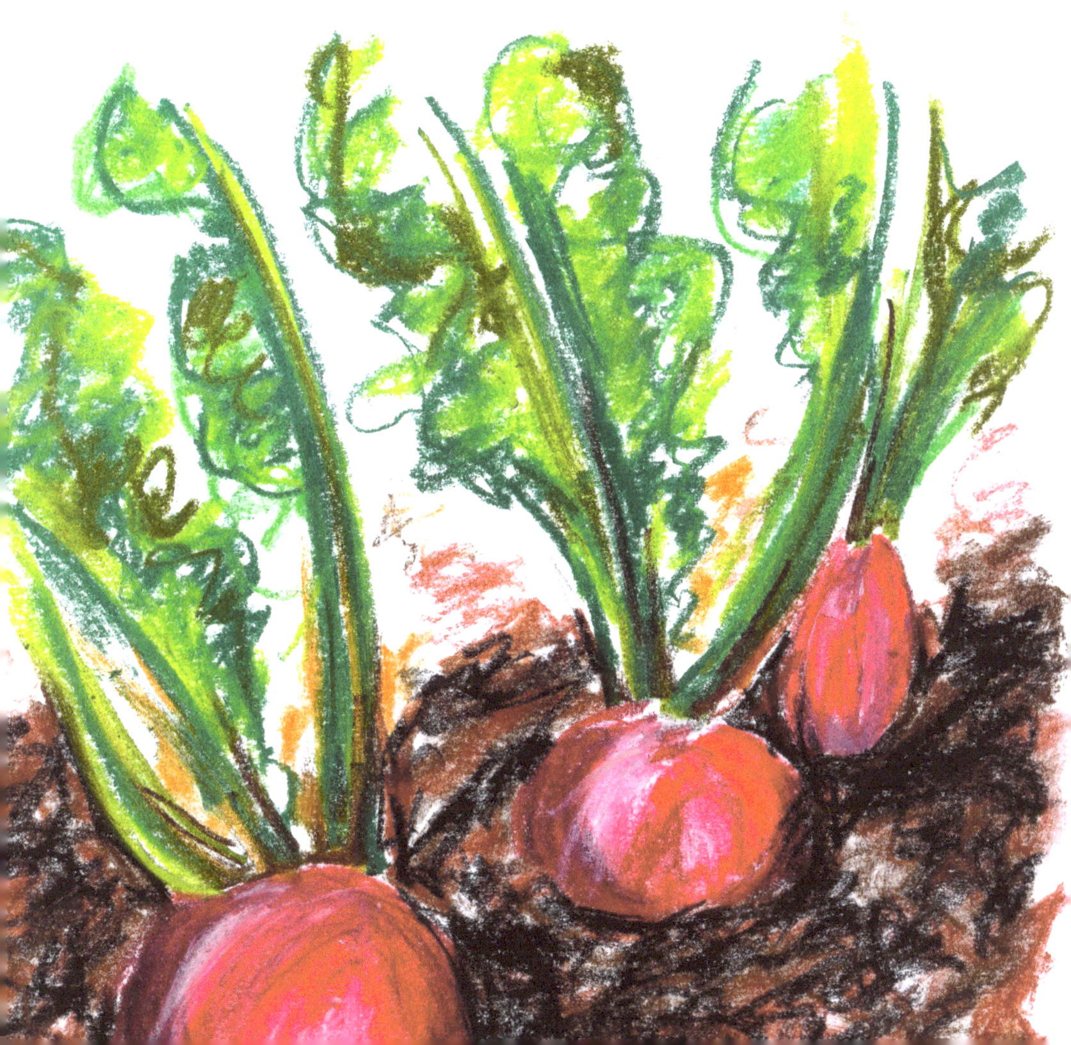

Cecelia's Creative Counsel: Plant the seeds. Grow your imagination.

Do you have a BIG vision? Similar to germinating seeds, the risks are high and results not guaranteed.

Failure is imminent. It is wise to break it down into stages while still staying committed to your long-term goal.

Baby Carrots story is focused on the early stages of any project, which are not glamorous: Preparation, Patience, and Nurturing.

Committing yourself to the end-result.

"*Look! Look, a carrot! Can I eat it? Please!*" Joann exclaimed. Releasing the carrot to Mom's hands, Cecelia washed the dirt away, "*Here ya go, ready.*" One bite, second bite, it was gone.

The small garden didn't produce much and the vegetables were all so small in size. But they were large enough to be included in Cecelia's delicious potato salad. Mom told everyone the carrots, green onions and radishes were from "*Joann's Garden*", I blushed with modest pride during the family dinner.

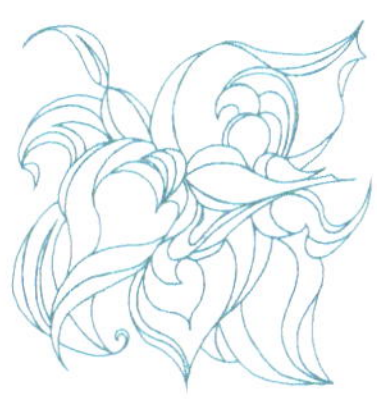

WET WRAP

Lilac season IS spring. The distinctive color and gentle aroma are the epitome of springtime. Beware: Make sure your senses are prepared for that wonderful fragrance during those two weeks in early may, otherwise you might miss it.

Our house was in bloom, inside and out. The backyard fence was a wall of lilacs. Vases, with cut stems, appeared in the kitchen, living room, and bedrooms. Spring certainly was an especially splendid time of year at our house.

Neighbors would regularly stop by for morning coffee. They came to catch up on all the neighborhood news and left with an empty cup and handful of fresh cut lilacs. Cecelia humbly accepted profuse compliments for the gift she had given and blushed with the effusive praise.

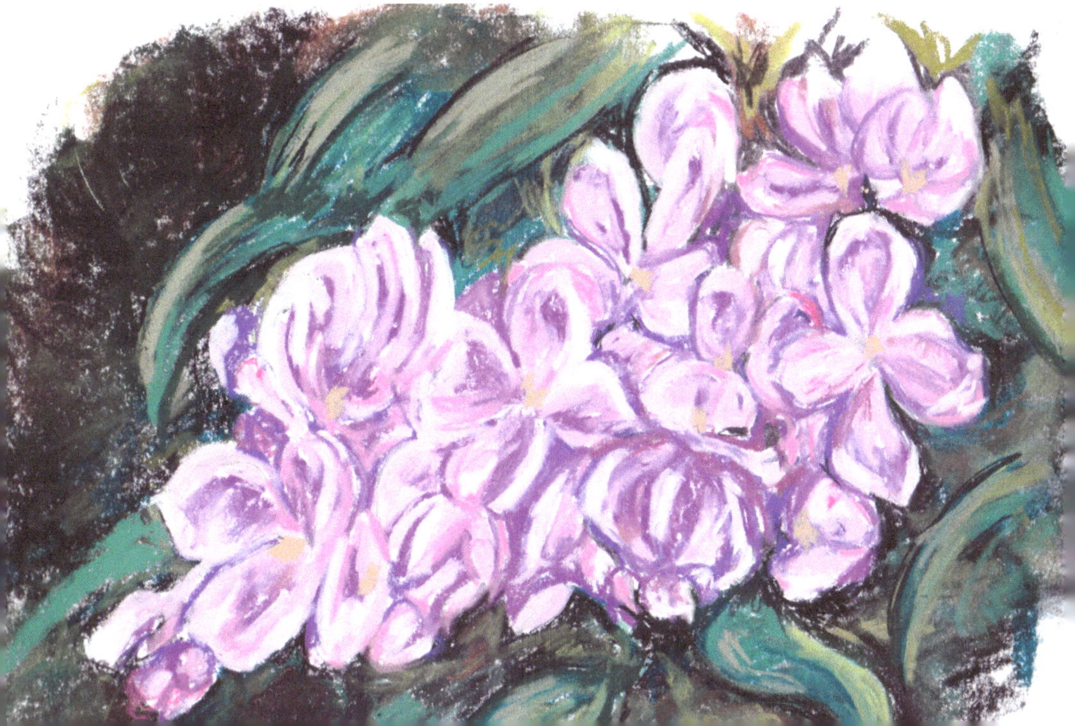

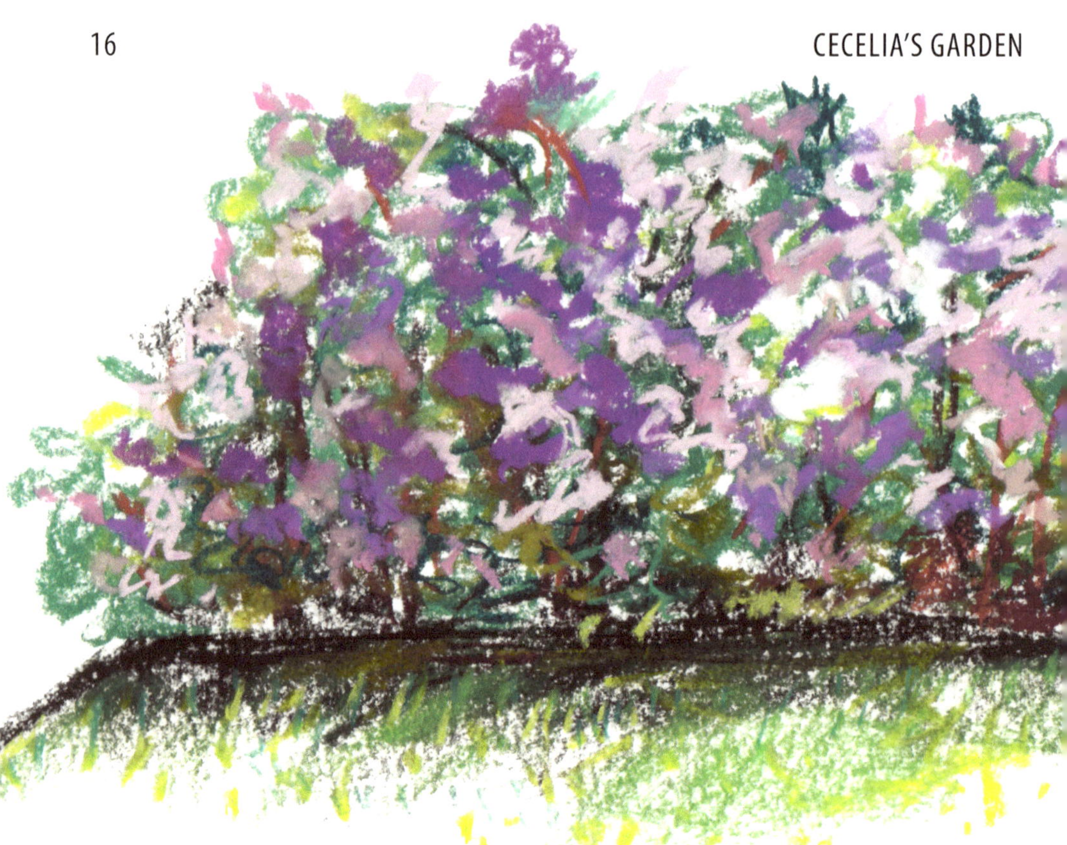

The backyard fence became a wall of lilacs every May. The wall reached its zenith with various shades of purple and white lilac flowers. The lilac blossoms contrasted against the heart-shaped dark green leaves.

When the buds first appeared, in late April or early May, preceding the explosion of color and fragrance that inevitably followed. This natural wall of lilac shrubs would mature into a ten to twelve foot high natural border. It also disguised the hideous chain link fence.

Our grandparents, lived in the city. They would drive to our suburban house to celebrate spring. Pops, our grandfather, arrived complaining that we lived "too far out in the country'. It was only ten short miles (he didn't even need to drive on any expressway). Nineteen Mile Road had once, indeed, been "out in the country"; but with the expansion of Detroit's suburbs, farmland transformed into neighborhoods, schools, and shopping malls.

In addition to celebrating spring, the family gathered to celebrate Mother's Day and two birthdays. Pat and Joann, Cecelia and Roy's

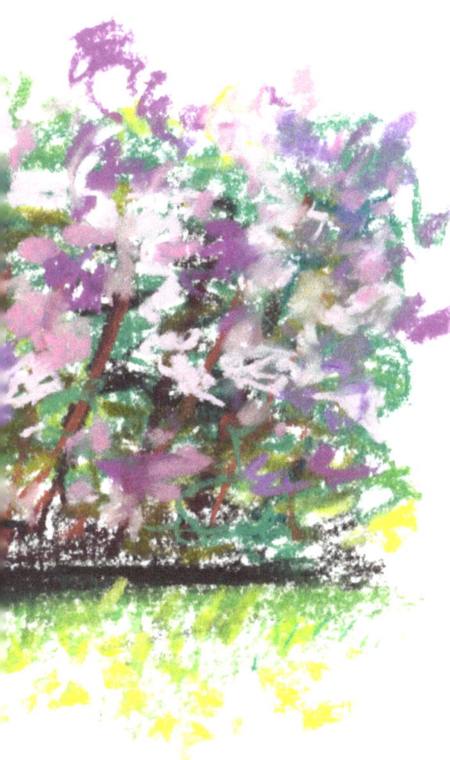

youngest daughters were born five years and one day apart.

Once the hugs and compliments were completed; our grandparents relaxed. They enjoyed playing with their grandchildren. Pops began tossing a baseball with his red haired grandson Brian. He was sort of special because he was the youngest child and the household's only boy,

The sporadic visits of my fathers' parents were always too short; a good time was always enjoyed, by all.

A walk around the yard was customary before our honored guests drove back to their apartment in the city.

Of course, an armful of lilacs was the ideal springtime gift for our grandmother.

Together, Dad, Pops and Neeny (our grandmother's special name) stood in silence in front of the lilacs. She paused for a long moment studying the lilacs. Gazing in awe at the huge hedge with all of its fragrant blooms. Dad stepped forward, with his garden shears, and cut the best blooms for his mother.

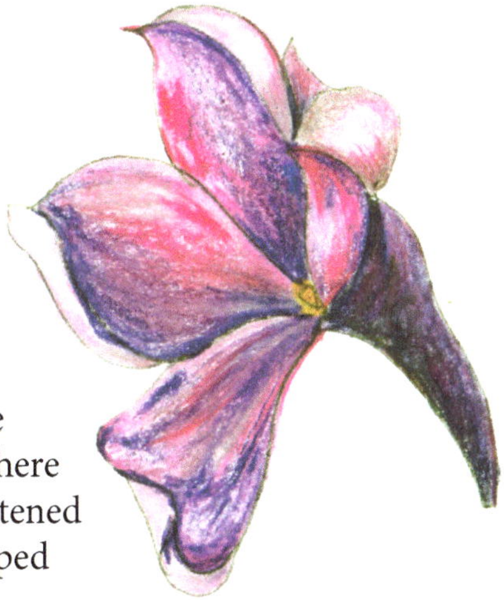

Roy and his father gathered the cut stems while Cecelia dashed inside to prepare her wrap for the bouquet. Her technique was the 'wet wrap'. This wrap was a multi-layer protection designed to keep the fresh cut stems from drying out before they were placed in a vase. The wet wrap consisted of a several layers. Everything would eventually be paced on a big sheet of white butcher paper. There was a layer of aluminum foil and Lots of moistened paper towels. The wet paper towels were wrapped

Cecelia's Creative Counsel:

Overwhelmed by an overabundance of ideas? How do you narrow your choices (or focus)?

In this picture, it is a matter of choosing the best idea at that moment. Knowing that there is an 'infinity pool' of ideas in which to return, again and again. Stimulate your ability to generate ideas and replenish, like the wall of lilacs.

Additionally, don't overlook the behind-the-scenes preparation to move your idea into reality. Layering one's skills and materials to bring it to fruition. Finally, presenting your 'gift' to the world. It is a gift and should be shared, humbly and gratefully.

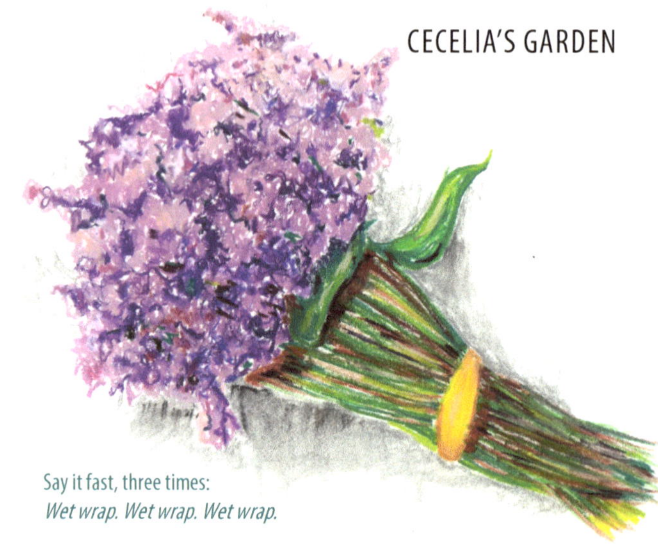

Say it fast, three times:
Wet wrap. Wet wrap. Wet wrap.

around the cut stalks and secured with foil. The bundle was wrapped with the butcher paper and conclusively secured with twine or ribbon.

The mega bouquet, handled like a newborn baby, was carried to the car as Neeny and Pops were giving 'good bye' hugs to their grandchildren. Cecelia passed the bundle through the car widow, where it was positioned on Neeny's lap for the ride home. All concerned parties were confident that water would not drip onto Neeny's skirt or the car's interior. When she got home, grandmother divided the bouquet among the kitchen, living room, and her dressing tables.

Cecelia used the "wet wrap" technique often. It came in handy when she was sharing any fresh cut stems from her garden. A method that continues to be used by the women in our family.

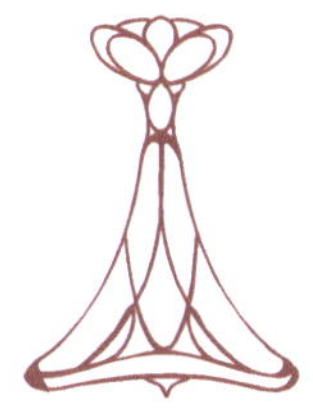

FISH HEAD FERTILIZER

In late March or early April, Cecelia's brother George, or her father would call to announce: THE SMELT ARE RUNNING. It was a clarion call for Cecelia. She had to be *on guard* for the arrival of huge quantities of small silver stinking fish.

Cecelia's brother and father were outdoors men. They enjoyed fishing and hunting. The pair traveled to northern regions of Michigan, and even ventured even further North to the ultimate wilderness of Michigan's Upper Peninsula. They caught fresh lake perch and went deer hunting in the late Fall around Thanksgiving. Grandpa loved to tell his story about a 'trophy bear' he hunted during a trip in Canada.

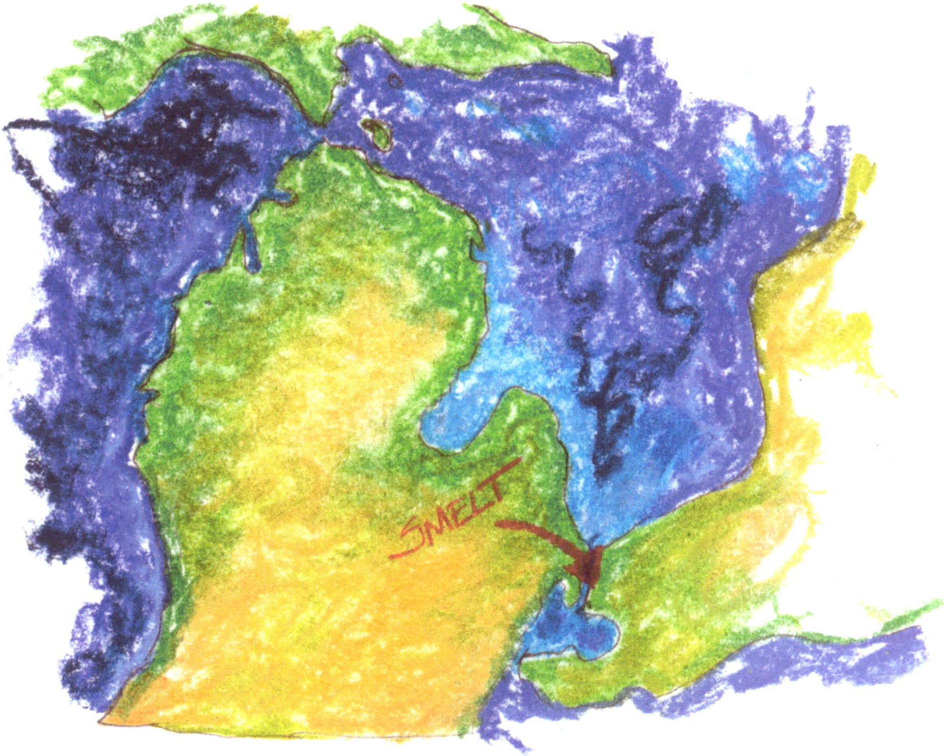

In the nineteen sixties, the smelt ran *en masse* in the Great Lakes. Uncle George and Grandpa went to their special secret spot in the Thumb area. Cecelia's rural heritage—her roots lay near Port Huron in Michigan's Lower Peninsula.

This dark, cold early morning, before sunrise, Cecelia's father and brother would 'drop their nets' in the shivering cold, shallow waters of the St. Clair River where it originates at the bottom of Lake Huron.

They filled their nets with hundreds of tiny smelt by wading knee-deep into the VERY cold water and scooped up buckets full of squirming fish. Smelt are barely larger than the minnows most fishermen used for bait. The individual fish may have been small but Uncle George and Grandpa's catch was quite large. There were always enough to feed four or five households. The fishermen put their catch into brand new galvanized trashcans that were eventually loaded onto the back of their truck. Each trashcan contained hundreds of live smelt and fresh lake water, the lake water kept the fish alive and fresh.

Uncle George or Grandpa would call, bragging about their huge catch and tell Cecelia when to expect their arrival. Cecelia, placed the phone on its cradle and immediately shifted into preparation mode. She ensured the driveway was clear of parked cars and toys, so Uncle George could back his truck up to the garage. They would move the galvanized garbage cans off the truck, lake water splashing everywhere, and take them through the garage into our backyard.

They drained some of the water and used a colander to scoop up small batches of smelt for cleaning. Their makeshift cleaning station was actually our backyard picnic table. Uncle George, Grandpa and Cecelia formed a production line. One person decapitated the little fish and passed it on to the individual designated to pierce the fish's belly and remove the guts and rinse them off. The last person used scissors to remove the fins and tail.

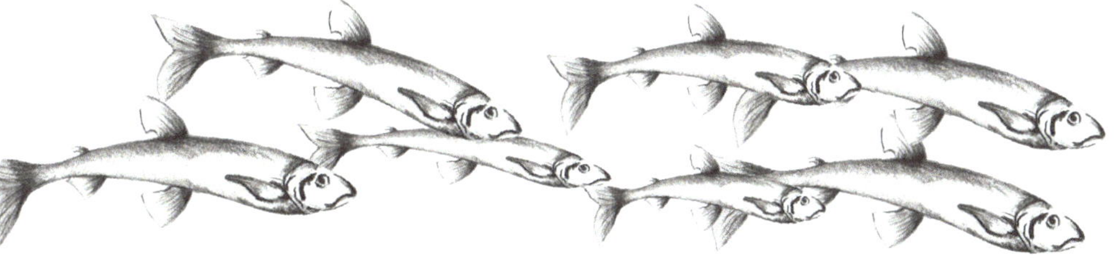

Another smelt was taken from the colander and the process, was repeated until they were all prepared for cooking. The process was repeated hundreds, maybe a thousand, times. When cleaning smelt, there is no need to remove the bones or scales. These fresh water anchovy are very small, and their skeleton is soft and digestible.

In full production mode, the trio worked together harmoniously. Each did his/her part of this annual ritual until the cleaning chore was finished.

Cecelia helped to clean the first few batches, and left Uncle George and Grandpa to clean the remainder, while she became *chef de partie*. Frying hundreds of the three-inch filets.

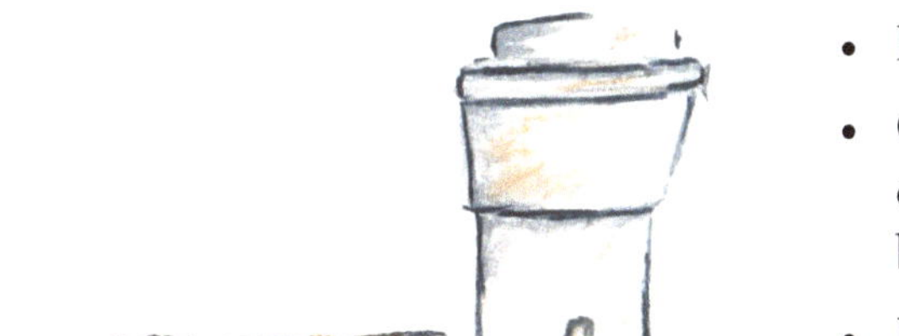

Her kitchen was ready:

- Dredging station,
- Cast iron frying pan carefully centered over the blue gas flame,
- Draining racks on the Formica counter, and,
- Finally, flattened brown paper bags on the kitchen table for cooling.

Along with condiments, paper plates and napkins.

Cecelia used a simple dredge of flour and salt & pepper, in a brown paper bag. It was the same mixture that she used repeatedly on a variety of foods. Grabbing a small handful of the patted-dry cleaned smelt and dropping them into the paper bag. She gently tossed the little fish in the flour, coating each one. Then Cecelia would remove the powder covered fish and carefully plop them into the frying pan with hot oil.

Cecelia was damn good at frying. (This daughter has avoided frying ANYTHING, except my sunny-side up eggs.) She would melt Crisco vegetable shortening in her coveted large cast-iron skillet. It was messy! Oil splattering everywhere, somehow she managed to keep it all under control. Cecelia even managed to have the remnants of smelt fish fry all cleaned up before Roy got home from work.

In her spacious, yet humble kitchen, Cecelia calmly deflected the distracting rush of activity around her while devoting her full concentration on the smelt frying in hot oil. Her fingers were encrusted with flour, her cheeks powdered white. Cecelia's clothes were disheveled and spotted with oil stains. Her salt-n-pepper hair was astray as she stood in front of the stove wielding her slotted spatula with practiced precision.

Cecelia orchestrated numerous batches of smelt through the cooking process, watching as the tiny fillets turn golden brown. When the little fish were cooked to crispy perfection, she scooped the fried smelt onto the racks, to drain and cool.

The final step was transferring the warm, lightly salted, smelt fillets to the kitchen table. A selection condiments, ketchup, mayonnaise and pickles, were on the table ready for anyone who cared to nibble.

The maelstrom of commotion, aromas, and debris, were all under the Cecelia's practiced supervision. She was the master of a work flow system that would have worked in any professional kitchen.

The smell of the frying smelt permeated the whole house. Thank goodness the open windows diluted the funky air. The strong smell of frying fish never quite went away. Despite our best efforts, the smell would often linger for what seemed like weeks past our special fish feast.

"Cecelia, what do you want me to do with the fish heads and guts?" Grandpa asked as he grabbed a few of the golden nuggets from the kitchen table.

"Leave it. I'll take care of it," she replied.

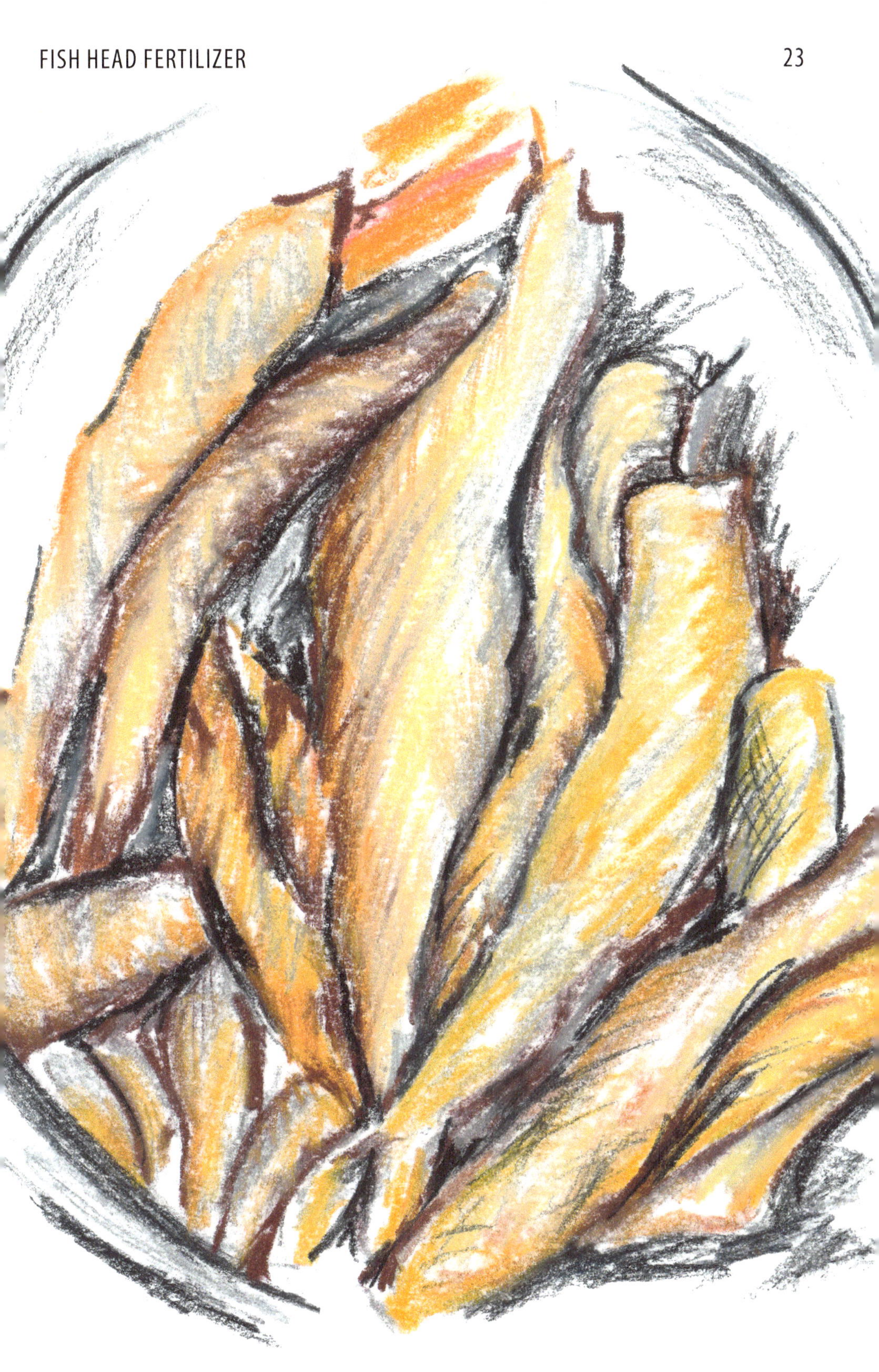

Cecelia's Creative Counsel:

Planning is essential.

At the spur of a moment, go into action. Establishing a process. The outcome wasn't important here, it is the process or work flow that consistently produced the best outcome for the team.

And, an offshoot creative lesson, be innovative with how to use/reuse discarded materials (or ideas) for another project.

Reclaim.

Reuse.

Reap rewards.

Cecelia saw the fish cleaning waste as opportunity for composting. The fish heads and guts would provide vital nutrients for her garden. Yes, Cecelia used the fish heads and guts for her lilacs, peonies and roses…*her little secret was buried deep down by their roots.*

She was reluctant to reveal her composting secret to her inquisitive neighbors. She guarded the secret of her success, like a master gardener. The result was a bountiful and blooming garden, with beautiful blossoms from early spring well into autumn.

In her efforts to involve the family in gardening activities, Cecelia 'encouraged' her children to pull unwanted growth, and weeds, from the gardens. On our knees, dirty and disgruntled, we would find a partly decomposed fish head! In a jolt, I would find myself up on my feet... sprinting into the house screaming in horror. Mom, sitting there reading or crocheting, calming replying, "*it's just a little fish.*"

Year after year, Cecelia's Garden produced an artist's palette of colorful blooms: white, purple, yellow, orange, red, pink against a background of greens; yet, it somehow DIDN'T smell like fisherman's wharf.

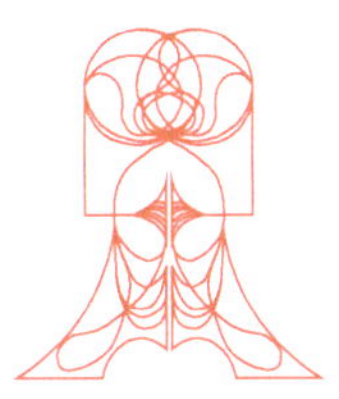

ROW AFTER ROW

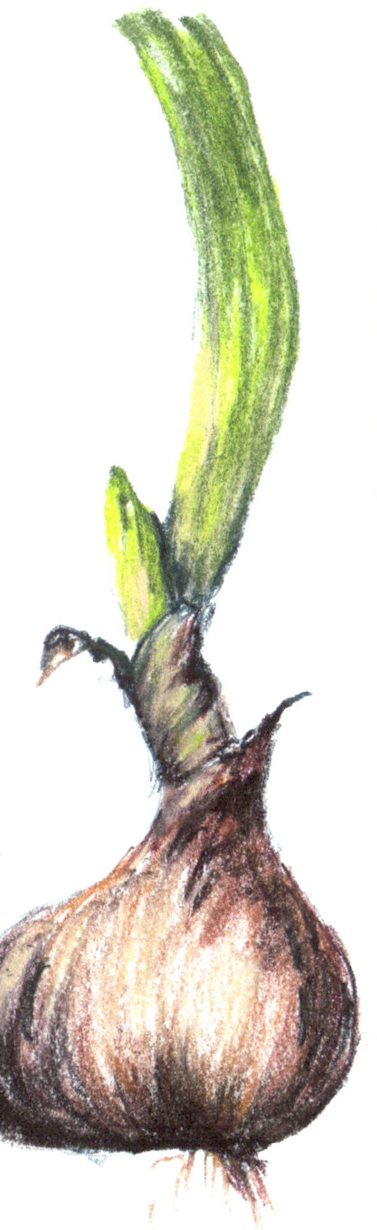

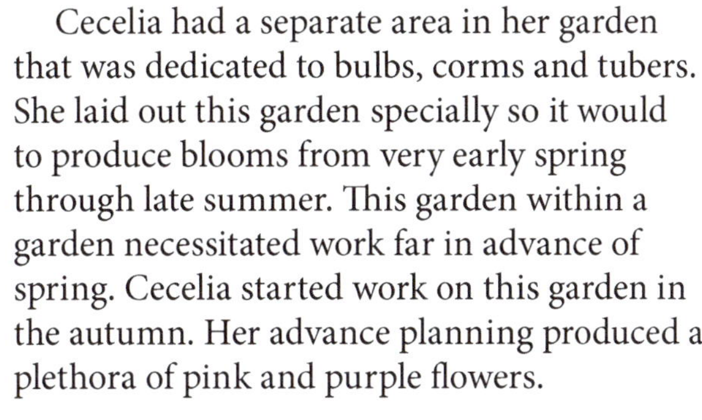

Cecelia had a separate area in her garden that was dedicated to bulbs, corms and tubers. She laid out this garden specially so it would to produce blooms from very early spring through late summer. This garden within a garden necessitated work far in advance of spring. Cecelia started work on this garden in the autumn. Her advance planning produced a plethora of pink and purple flowers.

This special high maintenance private bulb garden was not visible from the front of the house. It was her personal garden just for herself. This dedicated area was deliberately placed so it would be invisible to any passerby on the street. Someone might only catch a fleeting glimpse of it from the corner of their eye, as they crossed the front yard.

Cecelia's gardening skills incorporated the use of color, shapes and textures that defined this special garden.

During late September or early October, Cecelia began planning, digging and planting the grid of flowers that would lie dormant during winter, emerging in late March and early April and signal the end of winter. Once the bulbs were planted, the garden was protected from the Detroit-area winter with a straw blanket.

A master at planning, Cecelia consolidated her plan and calendar. She made notations in her *Old Farmer's Almanac,* tore articles from home & garden magazines, and put notations on her calendar. Cecelia also organized ideas on Rolodex cards that served as her version of a gardening journal.

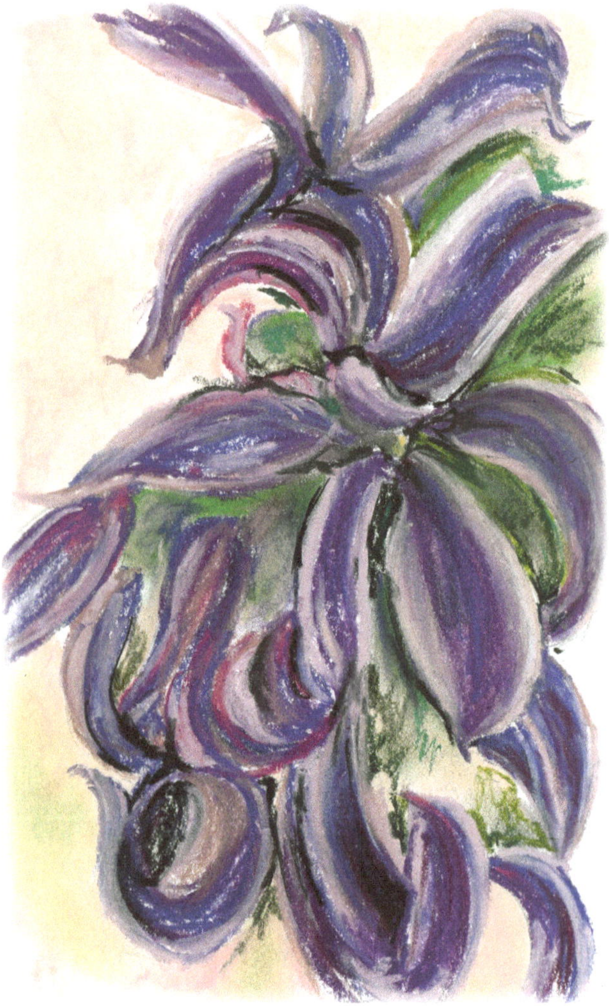

The complexity of Cecelia's bulb garden bed was multi-faceted. She structured this garden according to blooming cycles. Blooms would emerge while the last remaining snow was still on the ground and others would bloom through the end of summer. It was all laid out as a grid, based on the plant's height and color. The plant placement was well thought out, in terms of blooming order and size:

Hyacinth,

Daffodil,

Tulip, and,

Iris.

The first phase of Cecelia's plan began in the fall, before the first frost. She retrieved the bulbs from their summer storage and, adhering to a framework. Beginning with the first set, every successive set would take advantage of the blooming cycle of each flower.

First position, the hyacinth was planted at front edge of the garden bed. The short dome shaped blooms consists of smaller flowers with a VERY intensive fragrance. They were placed in colorful rows of purple, pink and white to alert visitors that spring has finally arrived.

Behind the hyacinth she planted daffodils. Rising in contrast behind the hyacinth, the daffodils' bright yellow and white displayed flower-within-a-flower bloom.

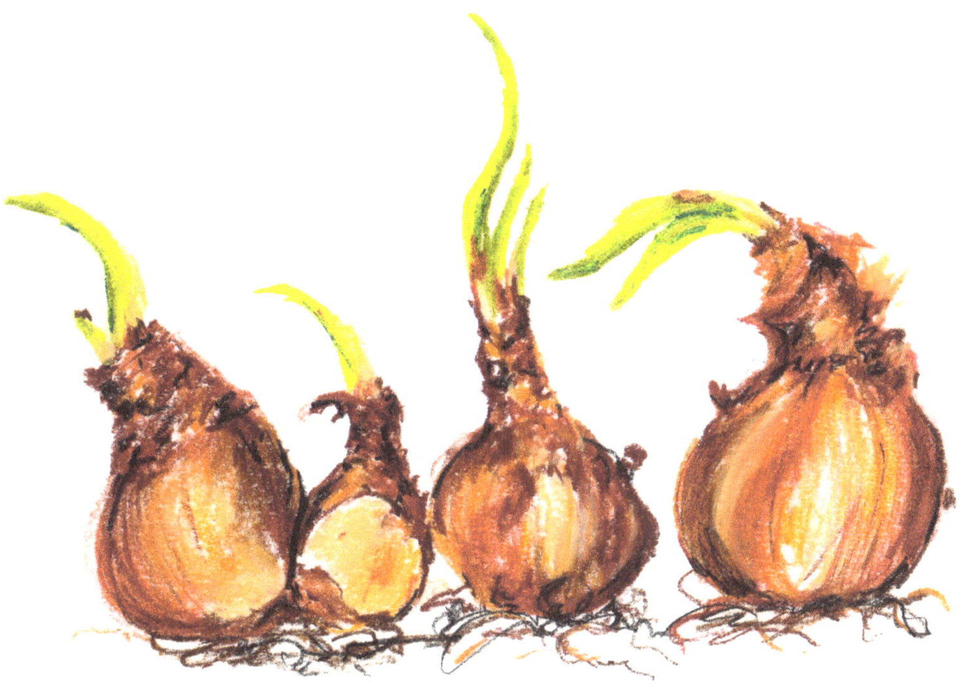

Next, rows upon rows of tulips were placed behind the daffodils. A seasonal favorite, the cup-shaped tulips filled the middle of the garden bed with a variety of colors. She planted red, yellow, pink and purple; a symbol of Cecelia's spring welcome mat.

The irises stood towering over the other blooms in the back row. Their rich purple, with a touch of yellow made a tall elegant backdrop for the preceding rows accenting their explosion of color.

The hyacinths, daffodils, tulips and iris became dormant by mid-May Their blooms turned brown and dropped onto to the soil. Cecelia dug up

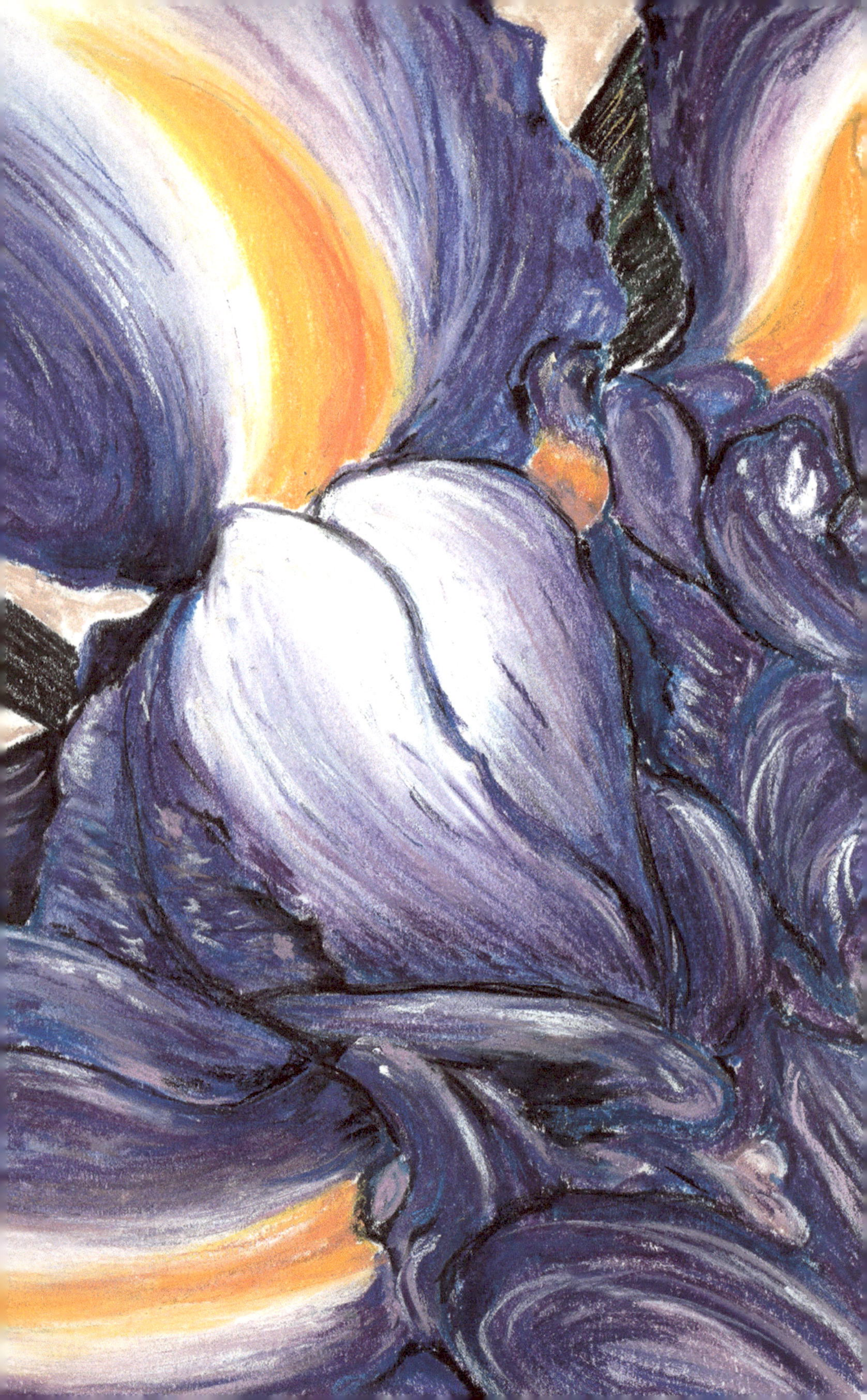

the bulbs and carefully prepared them for a long summer's rest. Carefully examining the bulbs, Cecelia wiped away any clinging soil and checked each one for damage or rot. Those that didn't meet her standards were tossed onto the compost pile while the bulbs that passed inspection were stored in the garage.

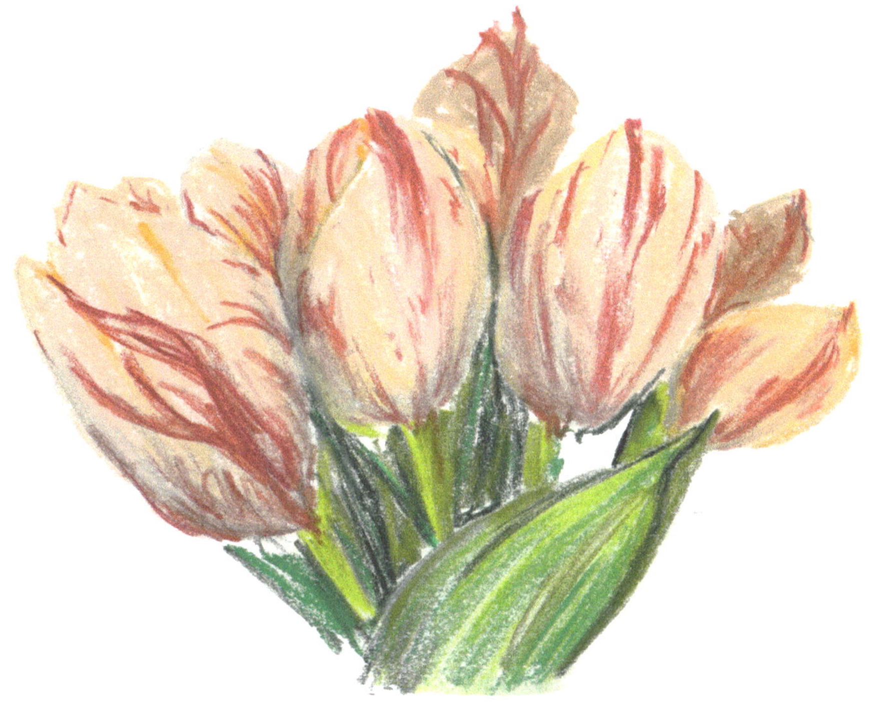

After Cecelia removed the hyacinth, daffodil, tulip and iris bulbs, the garden bed was prepped for gladioli bulbs. The glads were the finale in nature's cycle for Cecelia's bulb garden. They lasted through the end of the summer.

During summer, Cecelia filled the void in front of the gladiolus with marigolds, phlox and pansies, as a little something to frame the front of the garden bed.

Cecelia's expert planning and resourcefulness was evident in her gardens. Her bulb garden required attention and maintenance several times throughout the year. Her diligent effort resulted in a six-month display of vibrant colors.

Cecelia's Creative Counsel:

Practicing strategic creativity by recognizing patterns and developing a plan or system to take advantage of the pattern.

Planning is an important step in executing a creative plan. In this scenario, recognizing the cycle of growth of the bulb varieties for the garden.

Research the topic and/or data can help eliminate early mistakes. Learning from trusted resources. Extracting and applying the most useful for the execution of your own project/plan.

Experimentation is execution. The learn from failure stage. It must have taken a couple of years to perfect the system for this bulb garden.

Cecelia's research and experimentation produced months of blooming plants. Despite set-backs and occasional errors, she continued to research plants for their characteristics like height, color, care, planting time and bloom cycle and use this information to attain spectacular gardens.

She prepared the soil to optimize growth, etching her grid in the soil and dug the shallow trenches for the bulbs. She had organized the bulbs without mixing up a daffodil with a tulip. All of this behind-the-scenes work, that every dedicated gardener does, goes unnoticed by admirers of the display.

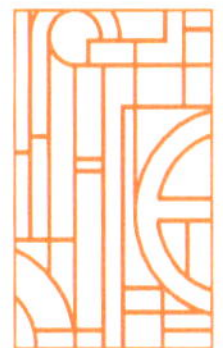

BACKROW OF GLADS

When the colorful display of hyacinth, daffodils, tulips, and iris was finished the bulbs were dug up and stored. Saved to be replanted in autumn…*it was time for the gladiolus.*

Continuing the explosion of color, the garden would be filled with gladiolus. A small front border of phlox and marigolds were placed in the front at the feet of the glads. All of this color and blooming cycle happened in this secluded garden, on the north side of the house, and lasted into late summer.

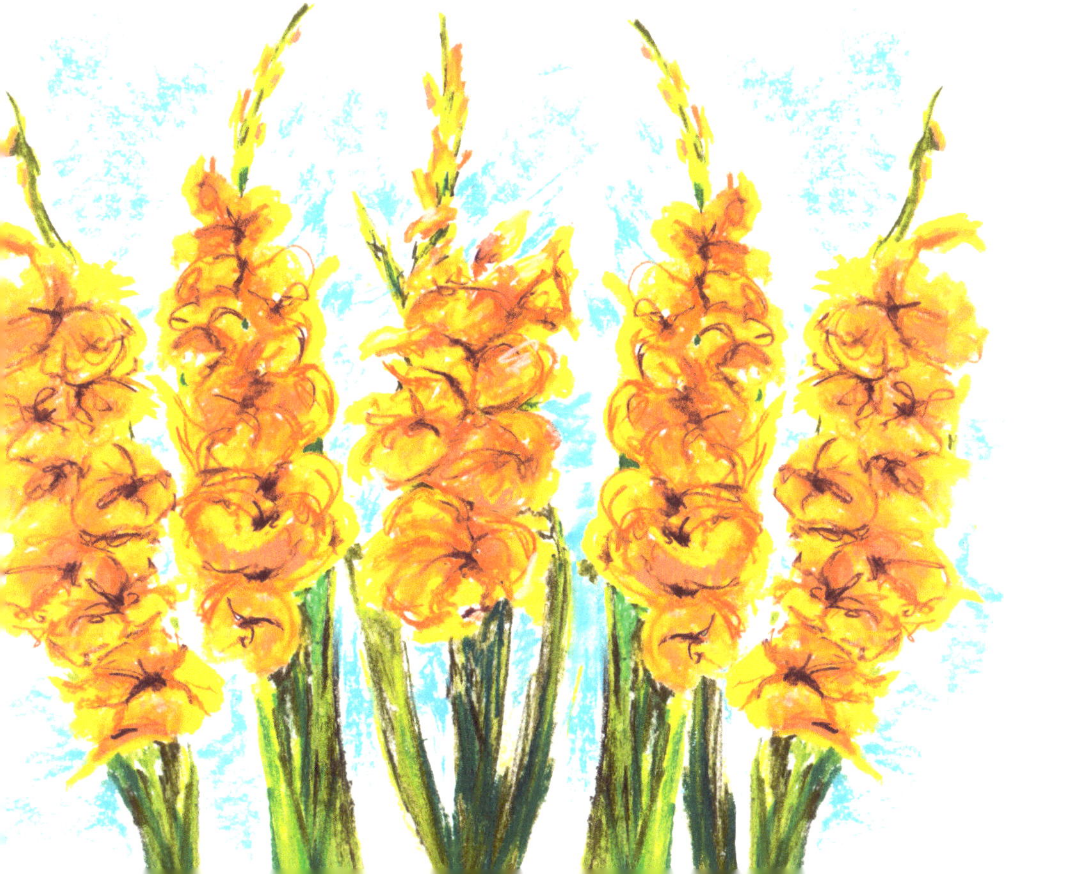

Despite the uncertainty of determining the gladiolus' bloom color, simply by looking at the bulbs, Cecelia continued experimenting with her bulb garden plan, Her gladiolus garden was bright with abundant vibrant blooms.

Cecelia's selection of flowers was her artist's palette. Her plants distracted from the boring and blah, beige vinyl siding on the outside of our house. She even accented the space between our house and the neighbors' garage. This area wasn't for child's play. It was Cecelia's garden.

Over time, Cecelia added new bulbs to her gladioli collection, replacing the bad or damaged with new varieties. Purchasing mesh bags of bulbs at the farmer's market or home & craft store; which she believed stocked the best quality flowers and bulbs and sourced directly from the grower.

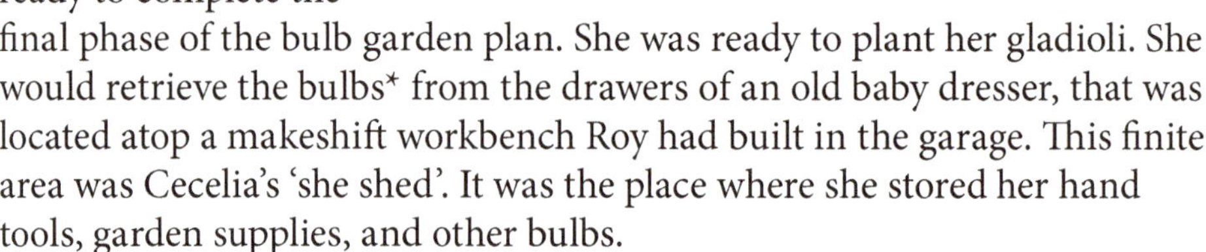

After spreading compost, in early spring, Cecelia was ready to complete the final phase of the bulb garden plan. She was ready to plant her gladioli. She would retrieve the bulbs* from the drawers of an old baby dresser, that was located atop a makeshift workbench Roy had built in the garage. This finite area was Cecelia's 'she shed'. It was the place where she stored her hand tools, garden supplies, and other bulbs.

Dressed in her favorite green cotton housedress, and wearing flimsy canvas shoes, Cecelia emerged from the garage with a basket of bulbs, small spade and cup of black coffee. She marched toward the north side of the house overburdened and determined.

"Good morning" was the total of her quick chat with our next door neighbor Jesse. Cecelia was content to be outside with her morning coffee and assessing the work that needed to be done.

It was time to get dirty. Cecelia knelt down, ready to dig, first pulling any lingering weeds and debris.

The garden bed was three to four feet deep and at least twenty feet wide. Cecelia used a spade, or hand trowel, to dig the long four-inch deep trench that would become home the gladioli bulbs. Her shallow trenches ran the length of the bed, leaving about six inches in between rows.

Now ready for planting. Cecelia placed the gladioli bulbs, point up, into the first shallow trench. She placed each bulb a few inches apart, then planted the next row and repeated placing bulbs until all the bulbs were in the ground.

The bulbs were planted in a pattern that would allow for maximum growth and visibility.

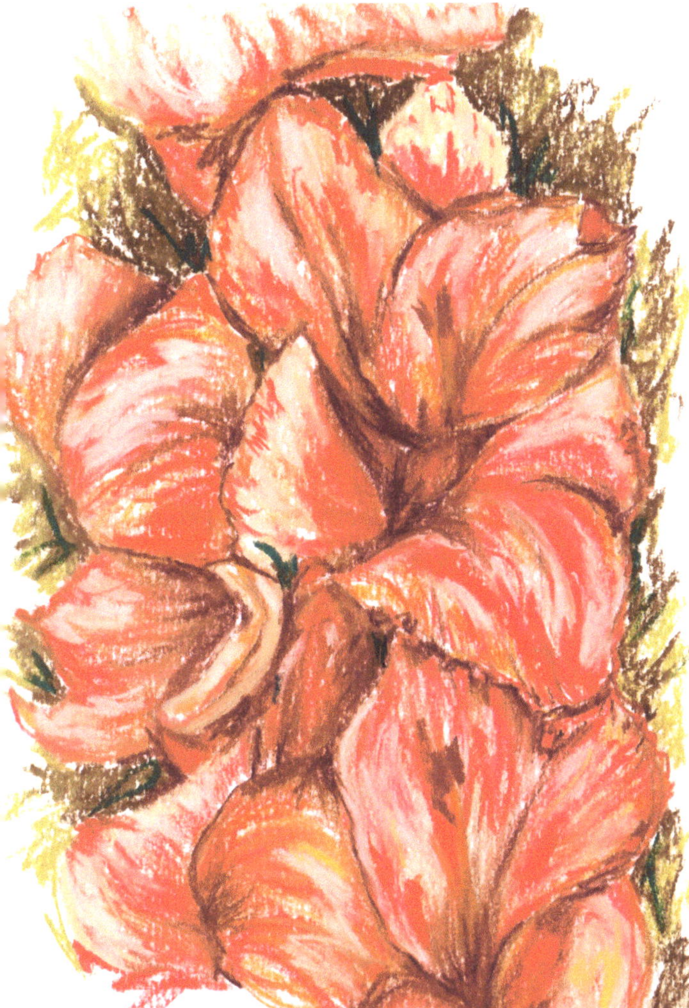

Once satisfied with the placement, Cecelia covered each bulb with soil mixture, gently patting to secure into position. The finishing touch was hauling the hose, opening the spigot and watering the entire garden.

It took about sixty days for the gladioli to take root, grow and begin to bloom. Cecelia patiently waited for the flowers to emerge. Cecelia was dedicated to her plan for her bulb garden; the end result was well worth the planning and dirty work.

Cecelia's Creative Counsel:

Once you have an idea, make a plan.

The plan becomes the system toward the end result.

The plan should include the concept and desired outcome, resources, tools, and deadlines/phases.

Also, the way that Cecelia did all the preparation of the garden bed and bulbs, factor in necessary preparation for each phase.

Having a system could keep you motivated, learn from failure and keep moving forward.

During full bloom the gladioli were tall and colorful: yellow, white, pink, red, peach and violet; their tall green stalks supported sword-like leaves. Tiny buds were clustered in small groups of three or four. The buds began to blossom and burst open starting at the bottom. They emerged in stages working their way up to the top of the stalk. The gladiolus were always in bloom for Cecelia's birthday in late June — like the moving music of a Main Street parade in her honor.

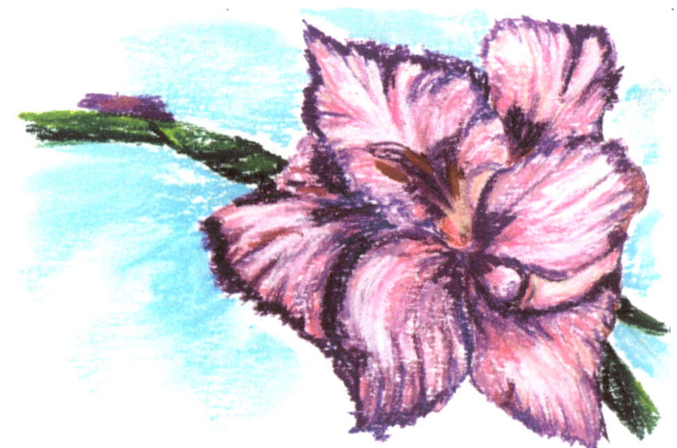

Roy often parked his car in the driveway and walked directly to the side of the house to cut a few gladiolus stalks. He would trim the excess leaves and shake his cuttings (to drop any bugs). Then walk into the kitchen, as if he had stopped at a florist on the way home. He filled a tall vase with water and gladili so the tall stems would be on display, for everyone to enjoy.

After the gladioli were finished with their towering show, Cecelia dug up the bulbs. She had to beat the threat of frost in late autumn. She brushed away any clinging dirt, flaking skin and unwanted roots from the bulbs before placing into the garage for winter storage. They rested, dormant, ready to be planted next year.

** Technically, gladioli are corms, because the roots emerge from the base, for convention, the word 'bulb' is used here.*

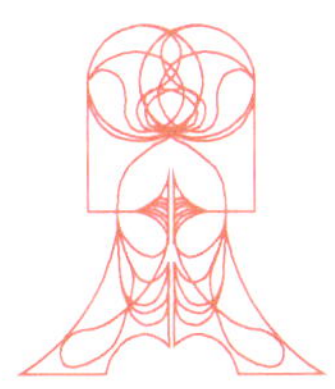

BURLAP WRAP BARE ROOT

Along with her playful and goodhearted nature, Cecelia was a traditionalist. She insisted on having a rose garden.

It was a modest rose garden that produced beautiful flowers every season. Cecelia cared for each bush with a certain passion, like it was one of her children. She monitored the soil and learned the characteristics and temperament of each thorny bush. Cecelia found that each plant was susceptible to disease and had unique indicators along with its blooming cycles. All of this individualized fussing yielded great joy and satisfaction to Cecelia as along with a bounty of classic rose blossoms.

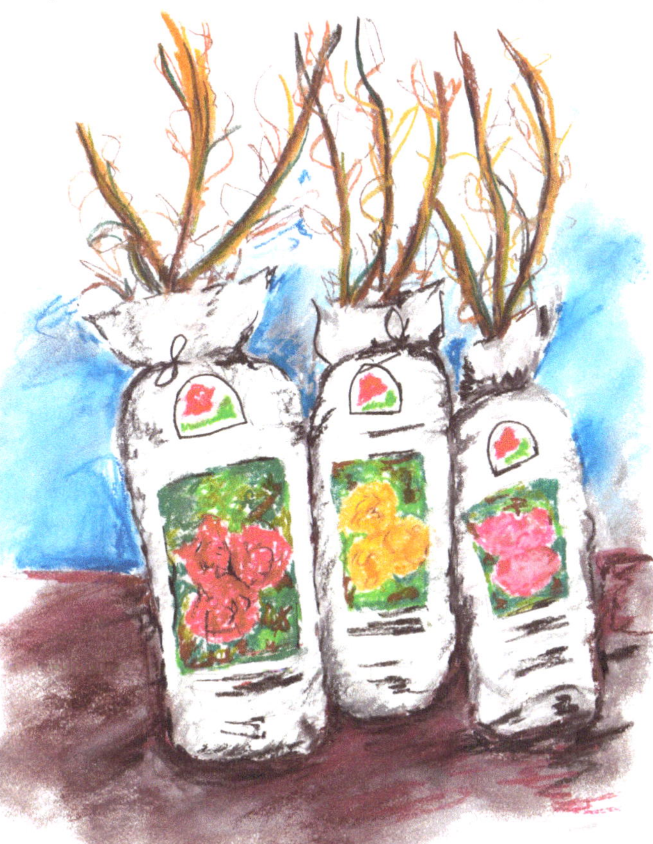

Mom would take a teacup with her as she walked along the dewy-grass edge of the backyard garden. She loved to admire her roses in the golden light. Her solitude in the morning was one of life's pleasures. Stopping at the honeysuckle in the corner, and turning to the right to walk along the peony garden she took her morning stroll as a humble version of walking in a formal English garden.

The additions Cecelia made to her gardens were deliberately planned, with an occasional indulgence in fanciful whims. Since she had an *unwritten* plan there was some flexibility when it came to a new rose color or additional varieties. Adding one or two bushes each season Cecelia replaced non-responsive growth and expanded her collection. Cecelia's rose garden was in a constant state of growth and development.

Cecelia had several trusted resources for her rose bushes.

One was the locally owned home and garden center. It was part of our family's Saturday routine and was a regular morning stop for all our never-ending home improvement needs. Roy would pick up the lumber, drywall, nails, tools and anything else he needed for his weekend projects. While he selected the best 2x4s, Cecelia would drift over to the garden department where she would shop for roses (or other plants).

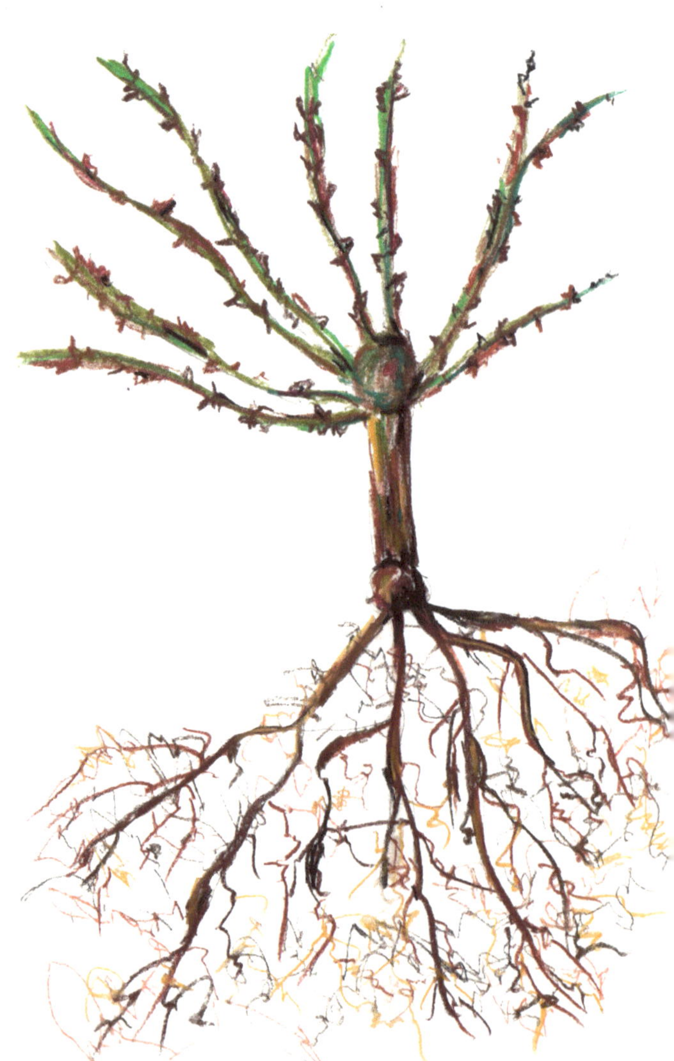

Another trusted source was Ben Franklin Nursery and Crafts. This store was like a department store; stocked with seasonal goods and craft supplies. A trip to Ben Franklin was always a trip that Joann was eager to tag along on. She had an insatiable list of necessary art supplies. While her mother strolled the gardening section, Joann would quietly wander over to the art supply section. Joann and search for a new paint brush, a fresh sketchpad or another tube of watercolor.

They drove home, in the turquoise Pontiac station wagon, with satisfied smiles on their faces...*creatively content* envisioning new projects. A burlap-wrapped rose bush lay in the back, ready for Cecelia's gardening artistry, and Joann clutching her new sketchbook. Cecelia had a plan for transforming her hulking leafless bush into a lush leafy mechanism that would produce dozens of American Beauty Roses.

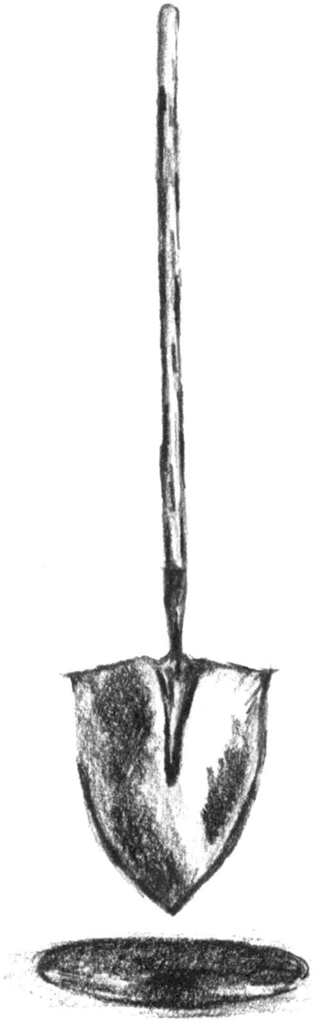

Cecelia hoisted the thorny bundle from the back of the station wagon and walked/dragged it into the garage. Cut open the burlap around the root ball and placed in a bucket of water. That bucket was the rose bush's home until the garden was prepared for planting.

"*You've gotta to see this,*" Brian got kick out of luring his little buddies into the dark garage to scare his friends with the sheer ugliness of this thorny monster. A prick on the finger and the boys would run squealing into the back yard.

Roy was actively involved in developing and maintaining the yards and gardens. His role was 'the muscle'. He dug the holes, moved dirt, lugged the hose, and disposed of debris. Roy also expertly trimmed a straight edge defining the garden from the lawn.

Roy excavated the hole, added Cecelia's seasonal *d' jour* compost for the roses, and added an enormous amount of water. He had made a sizable muddy hole. Roy grab would eventually seize the thorny branches of the rose bush, with his gloved hands, and hold the thorny beast study while Cecelia pruned the plant's roots and branches. When she was done Mom would squeeze

Cecelia's Creative Counsel:

Be unconventional.

Stretch your imagination
to achieve the impossible.
Your ideas may seem "crazy".
Innovation followed by action,
produce unexpected and
surprising results.

When you explore different methods (tools, materials, sequencing) you're using Divergent Thinking.

Break free of the traditional. Be prepared to break ground with a fresh approach.

"Was it as 'scary' as you perceived it to be?"

the roots together, in preparation for moving the thorny bush to its new home in the big muddy hole.

They worked as a team. Roy shoveled the soil into the hole while Cecelia, on her knees, worked the soil around the roots with her handheld garden spade. She worked the soil into all of the nooks and crannies around the base. Both parents tamped the soil around the newly potted rose bush. Roy pounded a stake next to the thorny monster. This stake gave the bush additional support and stability while it took root in garden.

During the summer, Roy would snip a rose from Cecelia's garden and bring into the house. Placing it into the milky white bud vase…red rose, a symbol of love. Love of nature and love for each another.

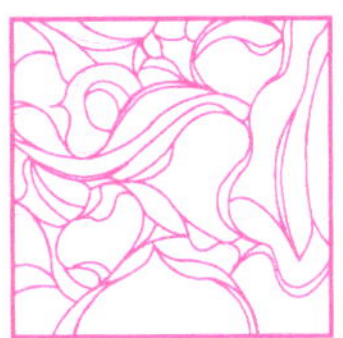

MILLER'S ORCHARD

Miller's Orchard was a working orchard with a true farmer's market. Miller's was destination for seasonal fresh fruits, vegetables, and plants, open six days a week, closed on Sundays. It was part of Cecelia's weekly shopping routine. She would bring home the freshest fruits and vegetables for her family.

Apples direct from the orchard, pumpkins from the Miller's own patch, flats of berries and cherries; paper sacks of peaches, tomatoes, onions, and potatoes filled the back of our Pontiac station wagon and pantry shelves.

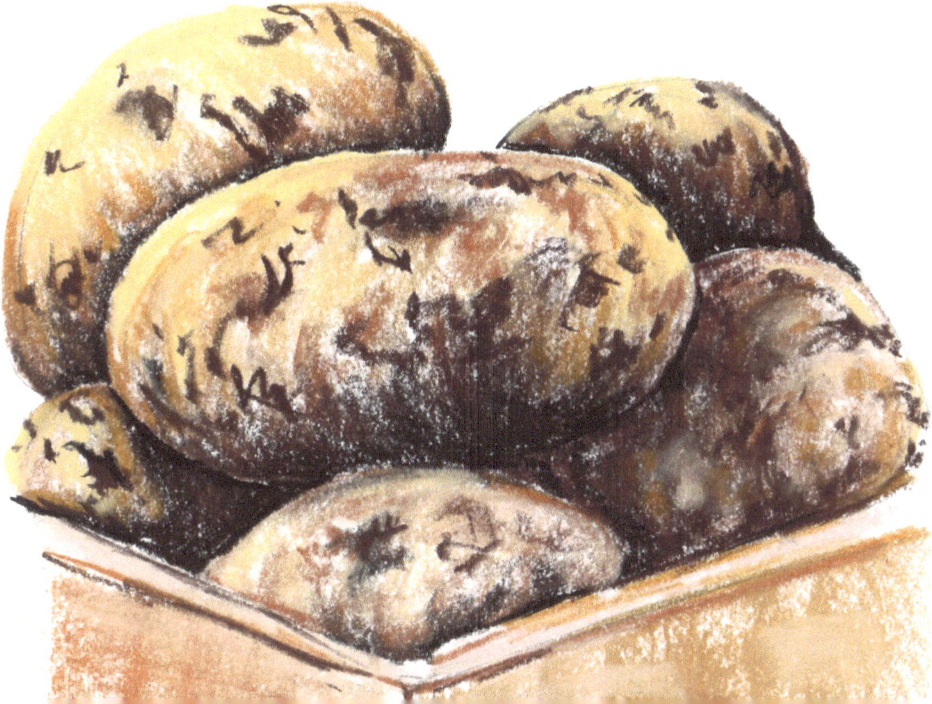

During the 1950s and 1960s the population rings, encompassing the city of Detroit, multiplied like the rings of a tree. New factory jobs and new housing attracted young couples, like Roy and Cecelia. They embraced a new lifestyle away from the once vibrant city of Detroit. Housing developments and neighborhoods replace one-thriving rural farmland.

Suburban living offered Roy and Cecelia a contemporary lifestyle that wasn't anything like their respective childhood experiences. Roy was born and raised in Detroit during a depression. Influenced by the curve from an economic powerhouse following WWI and conversion of the automobile manufacturing for war production had kept the city alive. By the time Roy was a teenager, the post war demand for new cars promoted even more growth. Thus, these economic stimuli created the rings of 'suburbia' around the city.

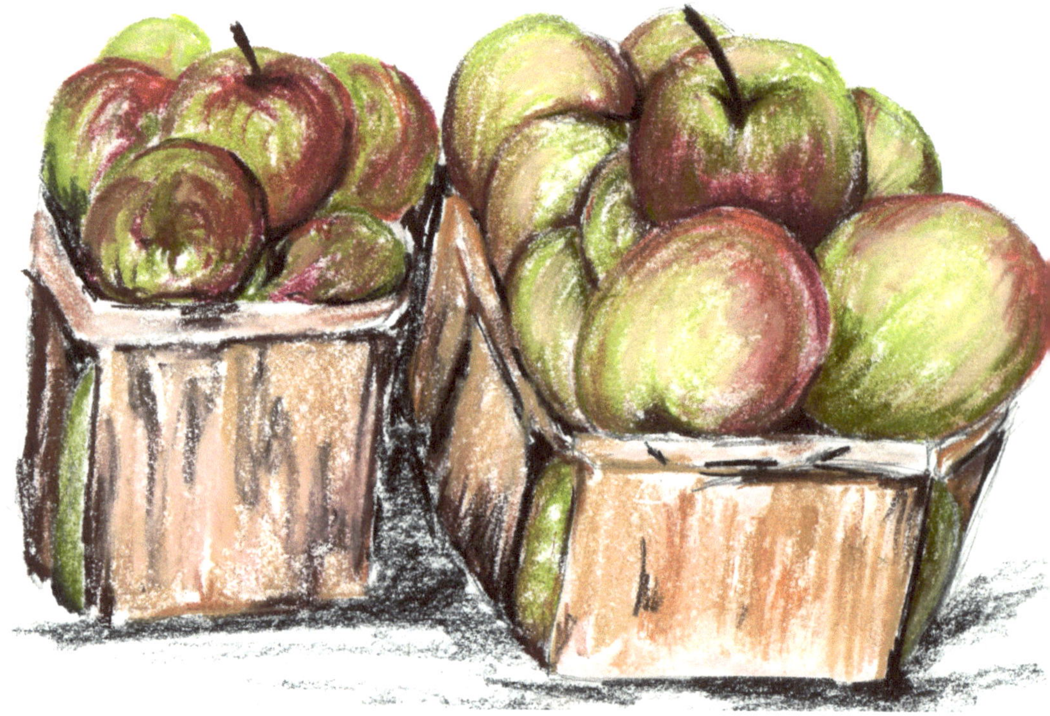

Cecelia was from rural St. Clair County, located in the 'Thumb' of the Lower Peninsula of Michigan, a culture and economy based of agriculture, family-run businesses and quaint Main Streets.

Our growing suburban area quickly developed any remaining farmland. During the mid-seventies the cornfield across the street from our house had metastasized into a new public high school. Joann was in its first graduating class. About a mile away from our house, a super-mall replaced nearly fifty acres of formerly productive farmland.

There were a few holdouts. The elderly couple, whose yard and field provided fun for neighborhood kids during our Halloween shenanigans, were there until I left in the early 1980s.

Miller's Orchard was (and still is) another holdout. The store was healthy walk away from our house with a worn path along Clinton River That was the was the same path we took to our neighborhood elementary school. Cecelia had *campaigned* to the local school board, city hall and school principals, for a proper sidewalk. She wanted the neighborhood kids to have safe sidewalks for their walk to and from school. Her hard work paid off while I attended Henry Ford II High School.

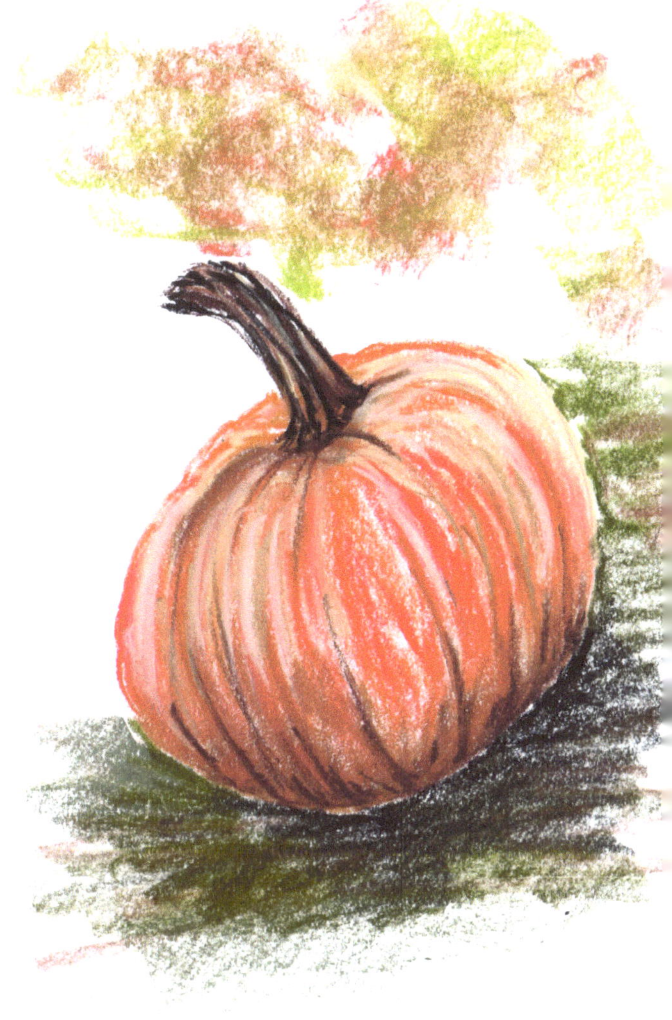

Miller's Orchard employed teenagers in the neighborhoods. They provided year-around part-time jobs (working in the store) or seasonal jobs working the farm picking fruit and vegetables.

Cecelia learned how to drive and got a driver's license. She was the first being dependent on her husband. Cecelia no longer needed assistance or have to rely on gaps in Roy's schedule. She drove to the unpaved parking lot at Miller's Orchard. If it had rained, we had to wear galoshes to muddle our way from the car to the front door.

"Hi, Cecelia, how are you?", a staff person knew her and greeted her as a valued customer and neighbor. Our frequent visits developed into friendships and deep-rooted connections. Everyone seemed to know each other. These relationships resulted in special selections among new arrivals, and better quality offerings for the store's "regulars".

During peak seasons, the station wagon would be packed with bags and boxes filled with dietary necessities for the family of six. Cecelia selected a variety of produce, appealing to everyone's palette. Mom didn't hesitate to include a peppermint stick, caramel apple or homemade jam for special treats.

Cecelia would also find seeds and plants for her garden at Miller's. She brought home flats of phlox and pansies to be planted along the borders of her various garden sections. Other items might be small foliage and begonias for the two concrete urns at the front of the house under our living room window.

Going to Miller's during autumn was the best! Fresh cider, even fresher warm donuts, caramel apples, pies, ugly gourds, corn stalks, and PUMPKINS! We also made the seasonal day trips to Yates Cider Mill in Rochester and the cozy country shops of Romeo.

Cecelia and Roy, *really* got into the Halloween spirit. At least four pumpkins were required, one for each of the kids (along with a spare one or two). A small mountain of pumpkin guts and left over pieces were hauled to the compost corner in the backyard. Of course, the seeds were rinsed, dried/baked and salted for snacks.

Cecelia made fresh apple pie from scratch. Her pie crust was light, flaky and butter-y smooth. It took me years to replicate her technique and attain similar results. Mom also helped us with homemade costumes for trick-or-treating.

Halloween was a big event in every suburban neighborhood. Groups of kids trooped out together. Older kids accompanied their younger brothers and sisters. Everyone all carried a pillowcase intending to have it FILLED with treats. Mischievous boys tried to intimidate the neighborhood grouch. The old pooh-in-the-bag-on-the-porch gag never ended well for anyone.

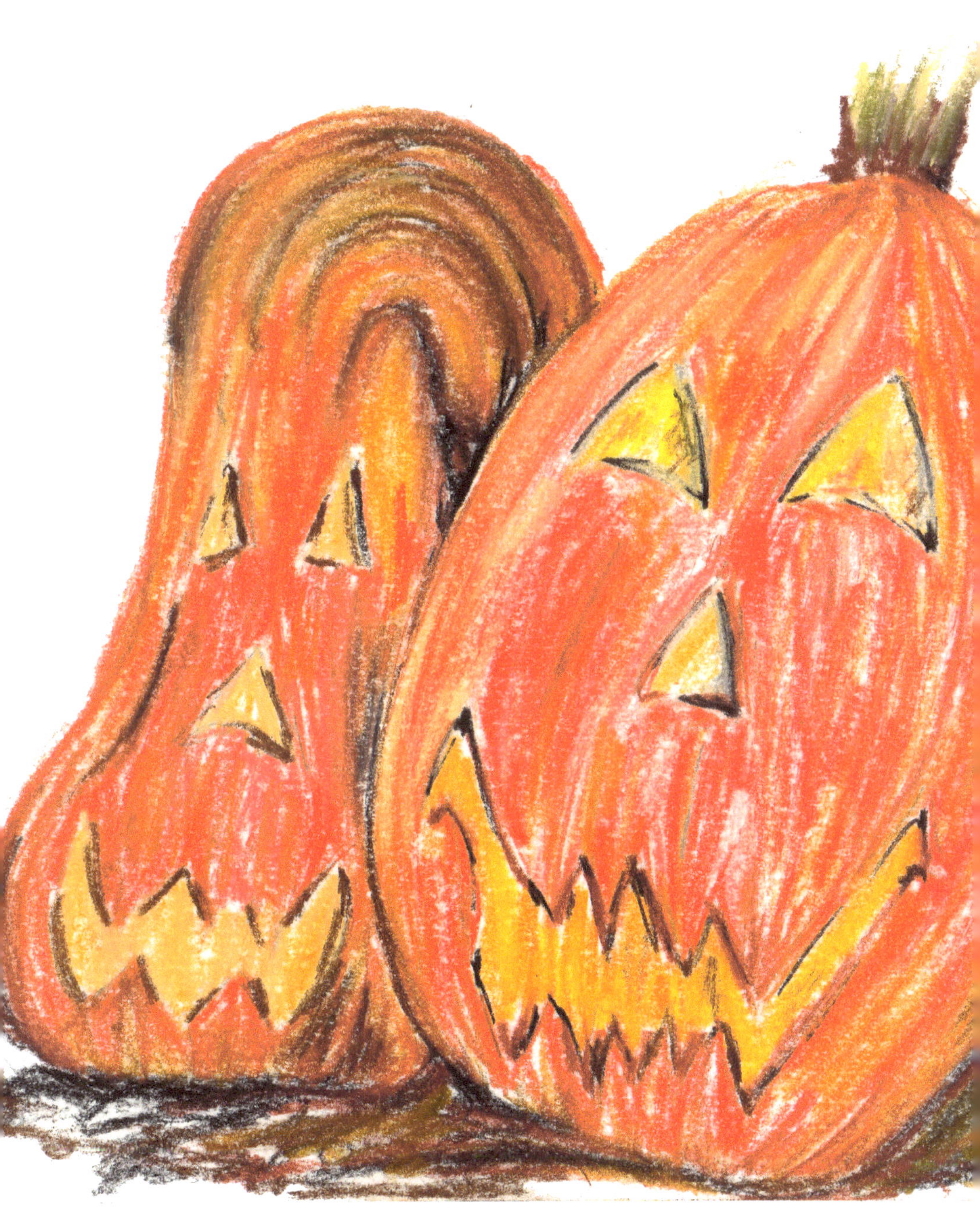

At our house, it was weeks of preparation that included the carved pumpkins, door and making window decorations, buying bags upon bags of candy and creating artistic homemade costumes. The hobo and ghost were popular and easy to assemble with items from the linen closet. We'd even fight over who could stay home with Mom to pass out candy to the first wave of costumed goblins.

Cecelia and Roy hosted a VERY popular adult costume party. Grownups dressed in costumes that were even more bizarre than those their children wore. Roy designed costumes that were so outlandish, that he earned 'the look' from Cecelia. Vinyl records spun popular music and drinks flowed into the wee hours of the morning while guests mingled and laughed. The basement linoleum was sprinkled with cornmeal and morphed into a dance floor. Buffet tables displayed Jell-O mold salads, cream cheese on celery and *Good Housekeeping* party hors d'oeuvres contributed by the revelers. Adults having fun celebrating Halloween, autumn would soon turn to winter, just like big kids.

Miller's was only open through December. Regular customers supported the local farmer by purchasing root vegetables. Cecelia picked up sweet potatoes for Thanksgiving, and, rutabagas for her mouthwatering roast beef Christmas Dinner.

Cecelia's Creative Counsel:

One of the most talked about creative problem solving techniques is "mash up." Take two dissimilar ideas/objects to create something new and different.

That's what Cecelia did. Relying on her rural upbringing and her new life, married to a guy from the city, living in suburbia.

Old school techniques helped keep it simple (KISS method) without wasting time and money. Reliable and, if it didn't work, adapt new technique, method or resource.

And, having a network of reliable sources for consultation, materials and support are fundamental to feed your creative endeavors.

PS: Playfulness is essential to cognitive creativity. Just ask comedic genius, John Cleese.

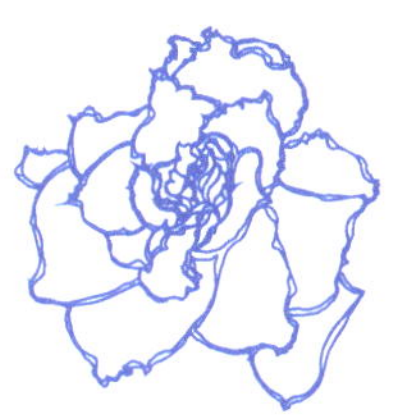

THE ORACLE

The annual *Old Farmer's Almanac* was a staple in Cecelia's household, as were *Reader's Digest* and *National Geographic*. These periodicals were essential reading and useful for reference.

The Almanac held a special honorary position in Cecelia's 'resource' kitchen cabinet. It was nestled in-between the phone book, recipe books, address book, coupon box, and calendars. Long before the internet, Google and voice-controlled technology, printed materials were indispensable for pertinent information.

When information was needed for a school project, or just to outwit Dad, we checked the *Encyclopedia Britannica* or *Funk & Wagnall's*. If we couldn't find an answer there, we would consult the *Old Farmer's Almanac*.

Printed with soft covers, the 200+ interior pages, on newsprint, were filled with useful charts, information and illustrations. The *Almanac* had

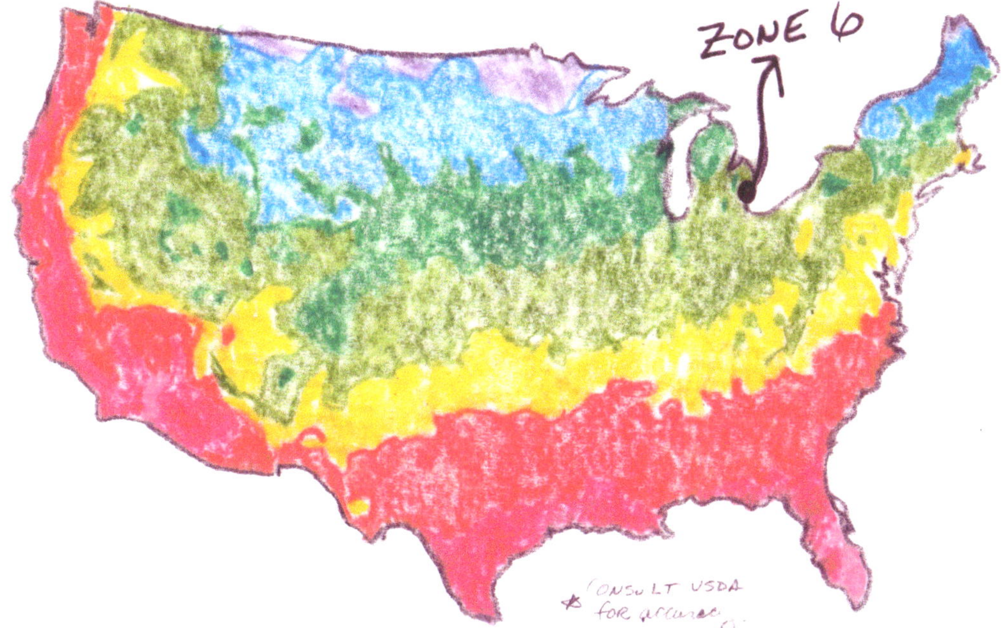

a sepia-toned cover that gave the *Old Farmer's Almanac* an antique look. It was like something found in the stale archives of the library or a country flea market.

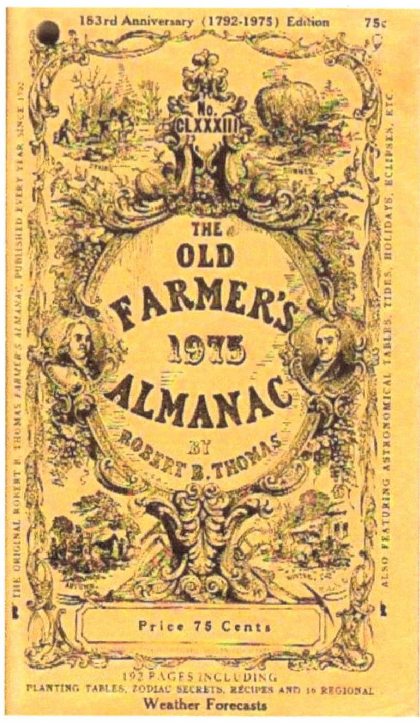

The *Old Farmer's Almanac* had EVERYTHING:

- Recipes.
- Lunar cycles.
- Weather forecasts.
- Gardening for all planting zones.
- Folklore.
- Astrology.
- Remedies.

Cecelia loyally purchased a new edition when it hit the magazine stand. The *Old Farmer's Almanac* was one of her most coveted, and stalwart, resources. It was more than a useful tool. The *Old Farmers Almanac* helped bridge her rural background, of two-track county roads, to modern suburban living.

Numerous times Cecelia explained how the Almanac was a fundamental aid. She found information essential to her with planting and garden maintenance and it was full of tips that were beneficial to beginners and 'seasoned' gardeners, like her self.

The 8x5" soft cover magazine was a treasure trove facts and figures. It was filled with incredible amounts of data and text. So much information, jammed into a limited space, meant that the type size had to be so small that a magnifying glass was required to read it.

There were descriptions about seemingly all varieties of plants, vegetables, herbs and trees. The best times for planting and cultivation

Nearest Climate Station	Altitude	Last Spring Frost	First Fall Frost	Growing Season
MT CLEMENS ANG BASE, MI	580'	May 6	Oct 11	157 days

were in the *Almanac*. Plus, seasonal care and pest control tips and end of season processes. The *Almanac* was consulted specifically for early spring frost customized for our planting zone; suburban Detroit 6A and 6B.

Cecelia's interests in gardening were primarily flowers, shrubs, and trees. She usually didn't propagate seedlings in little brown peat pots on the windowsill, unless her children had a school project or one asked about starting a vegetable garden.

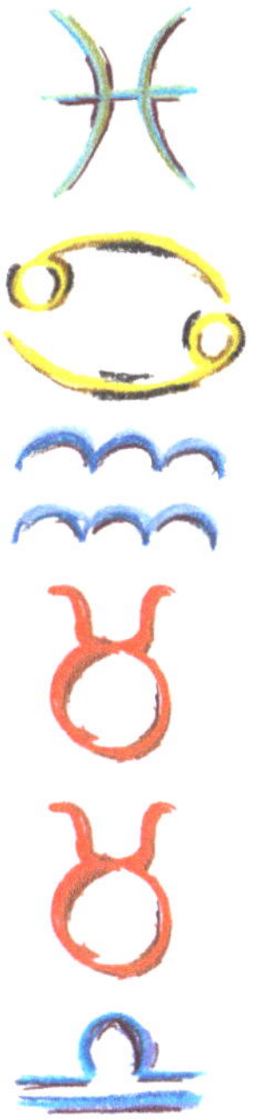

Interested in stargazing? Cecelia's *Almanac* was loaded with tables of astronomical data, dates and little moon phase illustrations for hobbyists, like Roy. The night skies in Sterling Heights were dark and the lunar calendar was in the *Almanac*. It was consulted before the family gathered around our telescope to stare at constellations or witness, up close, phases on the moon.

Beside consultation for the lunar cycles, reading one's horoscope was a form of birthday humor at the family dinner table. The *Almanac* was pulled from the cabinet and we would read our horoscopes, laughing at spot-on characteristics. No one was spared from the astrological forecasting.

The *Old Farmers Almanac* was placed back into its special spot in the cabinet, until it was needed again.

Cecelia's Creative Counsel:

Use lateral thinking by tapping into dependable and reputable resources.

The Alamanac is/was a trusted resource for a variety of household solutions.

This multi-reference annual publication has limited information. It was quick, handy and easy to digest. In-depth research and analysis did not exist on its pages.

A beneficial asset.

One of the seven core creative problem solving principles is limited information collection. Instead of burying yourself in excessive research, data and analysis you're opening yourself up to the unexpected.

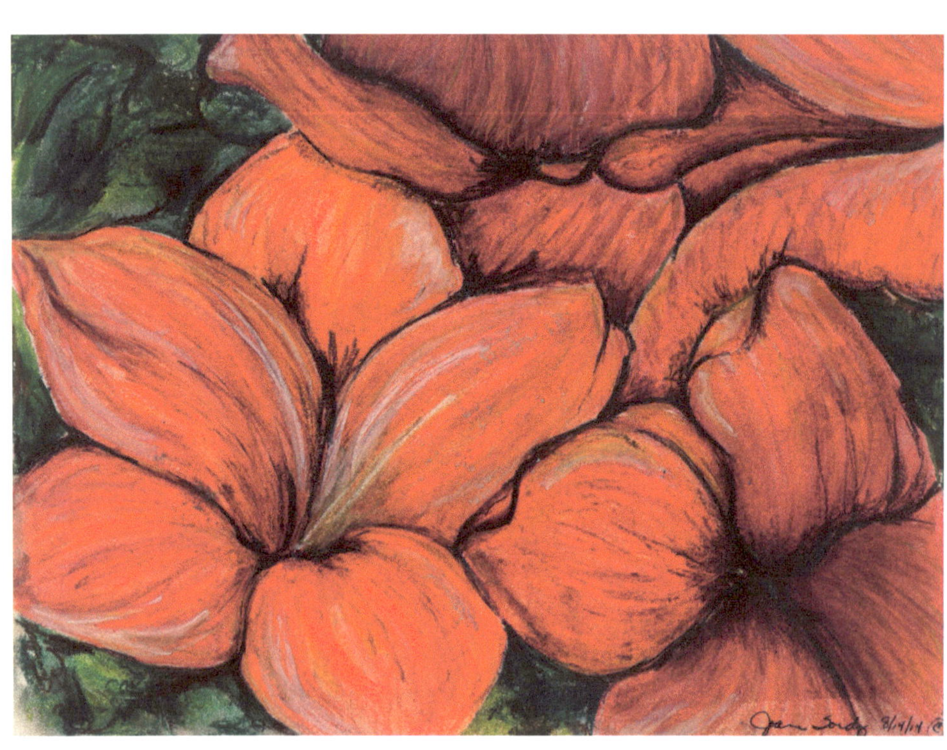

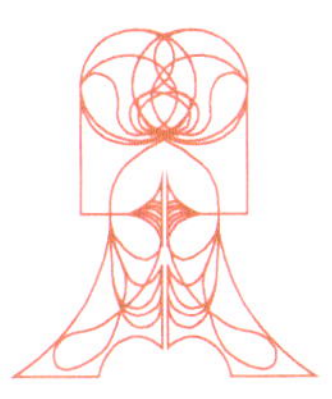

DANDY-LIONS

Managing a family with four kids, cleaning house, laundry, cooking meals, attending school functions & PTO meetings, helping with homework, planning parties, shopping, bowling league, non-negotiable Friday morning hair appointment... *busy*! Where did Cecelia find the time for her gardens?

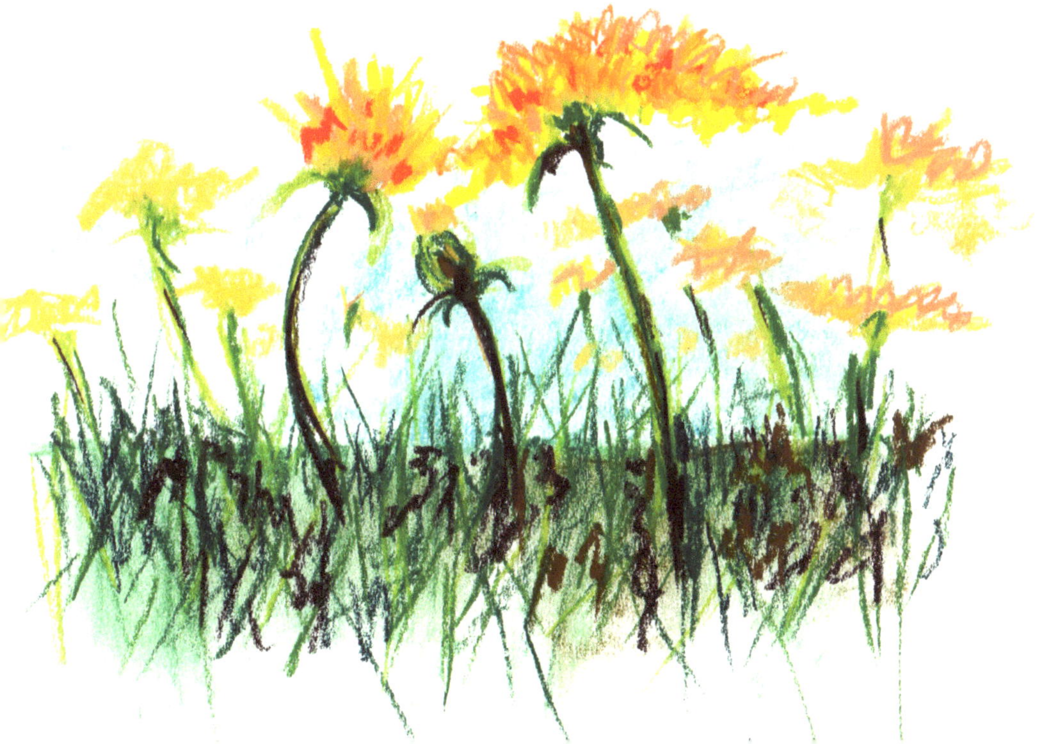

Roy and Cecelia were early risers. They were always up before sunrise; making pot of fresh coffee and reading the morning *Detroit Free Press* before the kids got up. If we did get up early enough, during summer vacation, we'd glimpse Cecelia outside tending to her gardens. She could be found kneeling on the grass, no pad or towel necessary, dressed in her favorite cotton sleeveless house frock. Cecelia always had cup of black coffee and hand cultivator at her side. She pulled weeds and culled dead

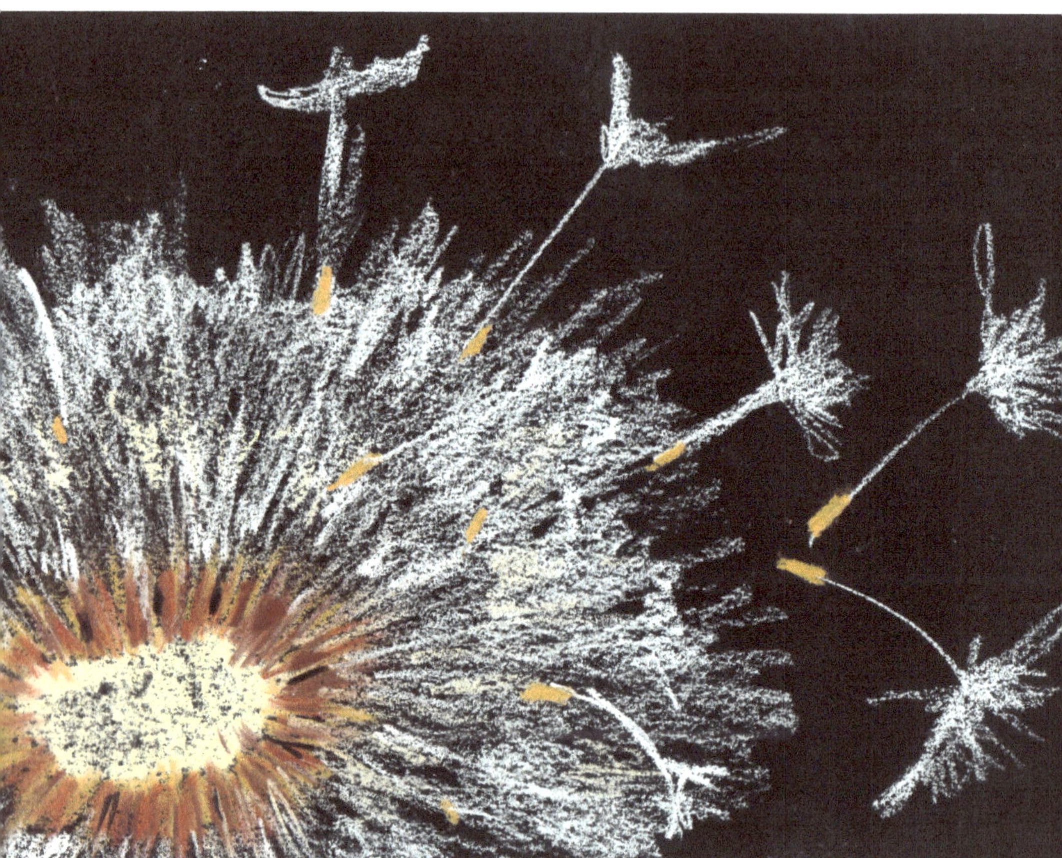

blooms off of her plants. As she moved along the side of the house and into the backyard little piles of debris accumulated every few feet,.

Cecelia's garden maintenance was meditative and meticulous.

One of Cecelia's most enduring characteristics was the importance she placed on the process of an activity versus the outcome. Accepting the flaws and imperfections were lessons for improvement when she attempted the next time. Her gardens were a reflection of this care and effort. They could be complete even with their imperfections.

It was common for Cecelia to find natural solutions to solve her gardening problems. For example: Cecelia's weed killer solution was made of everyday household staples. Vinegar, dish soap and salt were all she needed to combat a weed problem. In her garden shed there were very few containers of store bought chemicals. The commercial stuff was reserved specifically to feed Cecelia's beloved roses or ward off nasty bugs. She was more inclined to use the "natural" solutions recommended in her *Almanac.*

Our household, undoubtedly, had a do-it-yourself mentality. Budget considerations were also a major factor. Roy insisted on germinating his own front lawn from seed, while the neighbors indulged in laying sod. Spreading the seeds year-after-year, resulted in a lush lawn after about ten years of dedicated (or stubborn) work.

Still, Roy's lawn was not immune from weeds.

Brian was the youngest and only boy in our family. He and Joann were assigned the chore of eliminating the dandelions from the front yard. We would offer child-like curses to the blown dandelion puffs that came from our neighbors' yards. The coming infestation would later result in tedious work on a bright summer day when we would rather be doing something (*anything*) other than pulling up weeds.

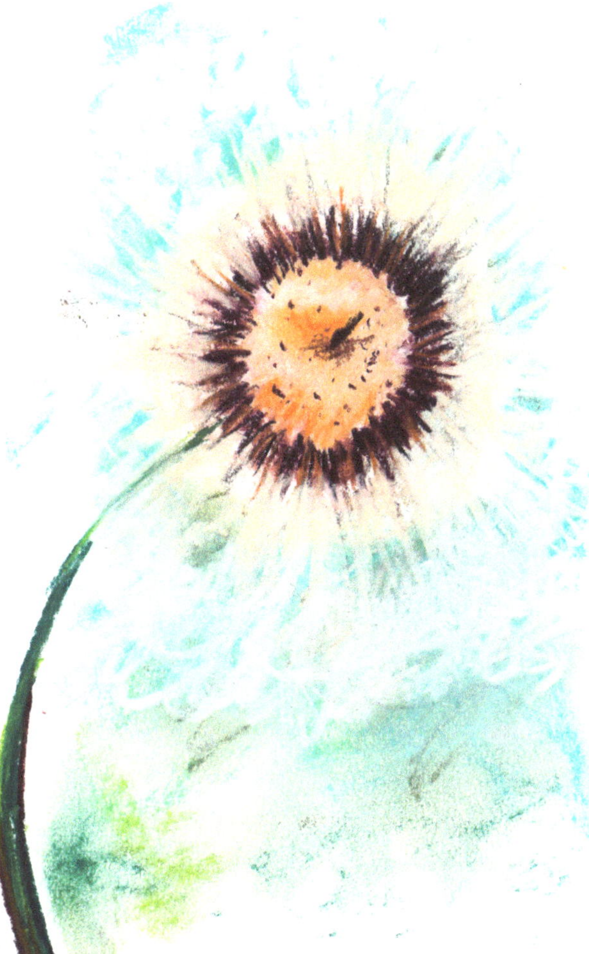

None of the tools in the garage made the task easy. Squat... pull. Squat... pull. The traditional fork weed puller was no help.

This was one of those chores that Cecelia took great pleasure to monitor. "*Be sure to get ALL the root. Or, it will grow back in a few days,*" she'd call from the front porch. *Yeah, right, Mom!*, keeping our frustrations silent.

Naturally, she was right. A dandelion would grow back if the ENTIRE weed,

Cecelia's Creative Counsel:

What are you missing?

What is hidden from view?

Can you 'go deeper' to take your idea to the next level?

Are there new or different resources to add to your toolbox?

Try a different perspective; afterall one person's weed, is another's flower.

including the root, were not removed from the soil.

There was one tool Brian and Joann begged Dad to buy: Grandpa's Weeder. Operated from a standing position, we wouldn't have to squat repeatedly all afternoon. Just push the three-prong cage into the soil surrounding the weed, deep enough to engulf to root, and lean on the handle. Yank! A dandelion, and its root, were extracted, terminated, dead and gone.

We wanted this quick method so we could complete this chore and get on with our summer fun. We wanted to be swimming, bike riding, or playing baseball.

Despite the persistent use of Grandpa's Weeder, the dandelions came back every year. Sometimes Dad would offer a little bit of help. Once in a while, Roy would apply store-bought weed killer (which he never put onto Cecelia's gardens).

It seemed that, no matter what we did the dandelion plague was inevitable.

Part of the daisy family, dandelions could also be regarded as a gift to a loved one. Small children gave them as a wish of happiness and promise of faithfulness. How many times have you been given the gift of a *dandy-lion* from a child? A thoughtful wish; from them to you. Little girls and boys joyfully plucking the little yellow flower, "*Here mommy, a flower for you.*"

MOUND OF MANURE

Springtime yard clean up and garden preparation was a ritual for the entire neighborhood. All hands on on-deck for tasks were needed for this task to be done. It was more than our family's affair.. No one on the block hired a landscaping crew. Children were the crew!

Cecelia didn't keep her garden maintenance routine simple by incorporating 'old school' methods. She didn't use cedar chips to adorn her garden beds. Mom was focused on preparation and growth.

Cecelia ordered a small truckload of a compost mixture from the local home supply center to jump-start her garden's seasonal growth,.

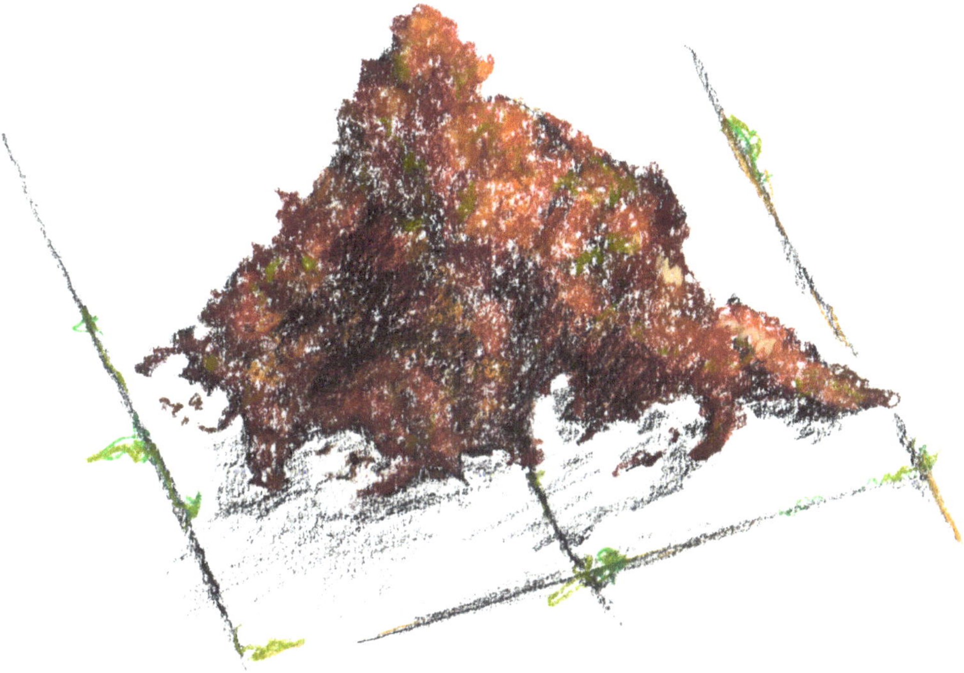

It always seemed to arrive on a clear, sunny Saturday morning. A small mountain of dark, dirt would appear on our driveway. After 'dropping its load the truck left our neighborhood, leaving a stinking pile rich black soil as evidence of its passing.

Cecelia found the pile, and its aroma, invigorating. The smell always ruined my appetite. My bowl of Cheerios, and glass of orange juice, didn't taste quite the same while that smelly black pile of compost sat at the middle of our driveway.

"I love the smell of manure, first thing in the morning."

Cecelia, stood in the kitchen. She had a big grin on her face; her eyes were bright with eagerness. Cecelia was in her element; holding her favorite coffee mug and proclaiming that *"everyone will be helping with yard work today."* We reluctantly, but quickly finished our breakfast. Everyone, dressed in work clothes, trudged outside like prisoners on a work detail.

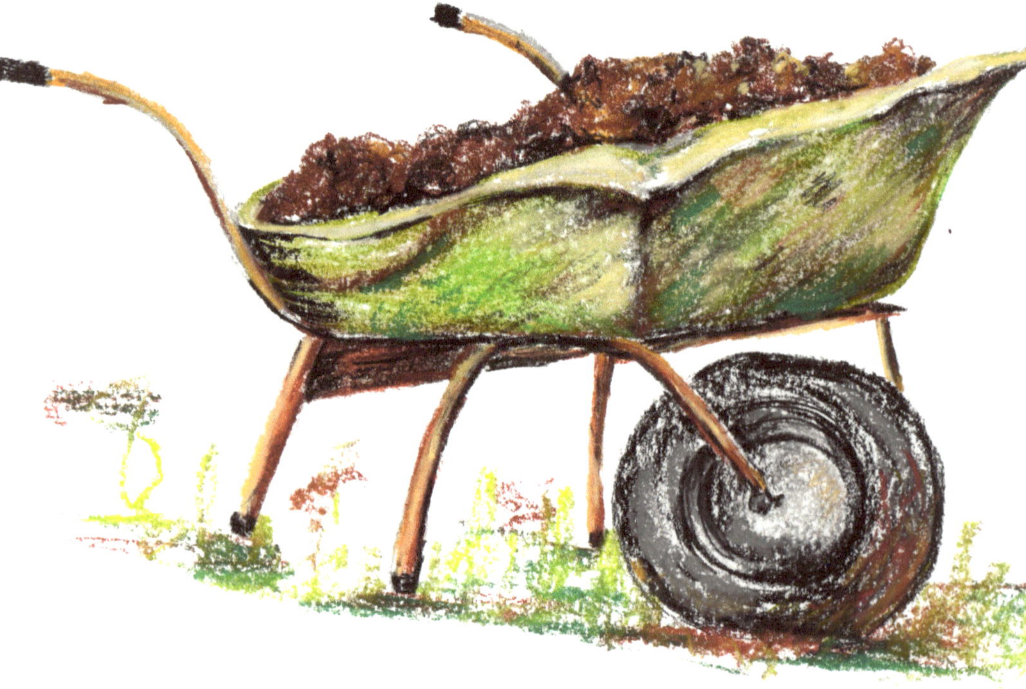

The work we invested today would contribute to the colorful bounty of gardens throughout the Spring and Summer.

Dad did the heavy lifting. He shoveled rich soil from the dark brown steaming mound into his wheelbarrow, wagon, and even pails. Everyone lined up to refill our containers. We were going to evenly redistribute the stinking stuff everywhere. Mom wanted plants to grow. Our small shovels had little impact on reducing the mound by lunchtime.

Shovel by shovel, wheelbarrow by wheelbarrow, the compost was moved from the driveway to the garden beds in the front and back yards; and put at the base of the trees and hedges.

Cathy and Pat, my two eldest sisters, were better at shoveling. They scooped shovels full from the wheelbarrow and sprinkled the almost black, dirt onto the garden beds. They were careful not to cover the emerging tulips, hyacinth and daffodils. Down on her knees and using a three-pronged cultivator, Joann spread the smelly stuff; most likely getting more on her knees and feet than on the ground.

Eager to help Dad, Brian had his miniature tools and little wagon working alongside his father, imitating his movements. Brian was tasked with filling the concrete planters on the front porch.

It was a new suburban development, no landscaped yards, just dirt when Roy and Cecelia bought the house. Over the years they painstakingly and patiently landscaped both yards with grass, gardens, shrubs, and trees.

Trees were planted representing each of their four children. Different kinds of trees represented the individuality of Cathy, Pat, Joann and Brian. The evergreen, chosen to represent Joann, was spared from the axe during installation of the aboveground pool in the early seventies. The older sisters' trees were crabapple and a fire thorn was selected for Brian...*just kidding*!

Dad always placed compost at the base of all the trees in both yards. The annual spring compost ritual helped sustain those trees for decades.

Supervising, like a construction foreman, Cecelia presided over the movement of the *gross merde*. She enjoyed seeing her family working together.

Cecelia held back her distinctive laughter as her children continually reflected, "*ewe, this smells like pooh*". Sweat, soil and sarcasm...were all part of this typical Saturday in our neighborhood.

Eager to get her gardens prepped for the year, Cecelia went into high-energy mode. For days preceding the "dump" she expertly planned her household routine. Mom wanted the housekeeping and laundry chores DONE and out of the way. Following her never-to-be-missed Friday morning hair appointment, she made traditional English pasties for Saturday's lunch. Her fabulous pasties were a family favorite. They made a great meal for lunch or dinner and were even a filling snack.

Shortly after lunch, Cathy would make a quick escape into the house. She *had to be* the first into the shower. Her reason: *date night.* (of course). Cathy had to fix herself up leaving the rest of us to finish the shoveling, raking and sweeping.

Everyone else's turn in the shower would have to wait.

Roy, working all day shoveling the compost, remained in the driveway. He cleaned away the remaining debris. By late afternoon, Dad paused to acknowledge his daughter's latest beau. As the teenage stranger parked in front of the house Roy stood tall (six feet-two inches) watching. His white T-shirt was blotched with brown, sweat dripped from his forehead, with his arm balanced on the handle of his shovel. No pleasantries were exchanged. Father gave his critical 'Dad look', complete with an arched eyebrow high above his icy blue eyes. Roy made a sarcastic "nice car" comment. "*Ready to go?*" as his daughter called,

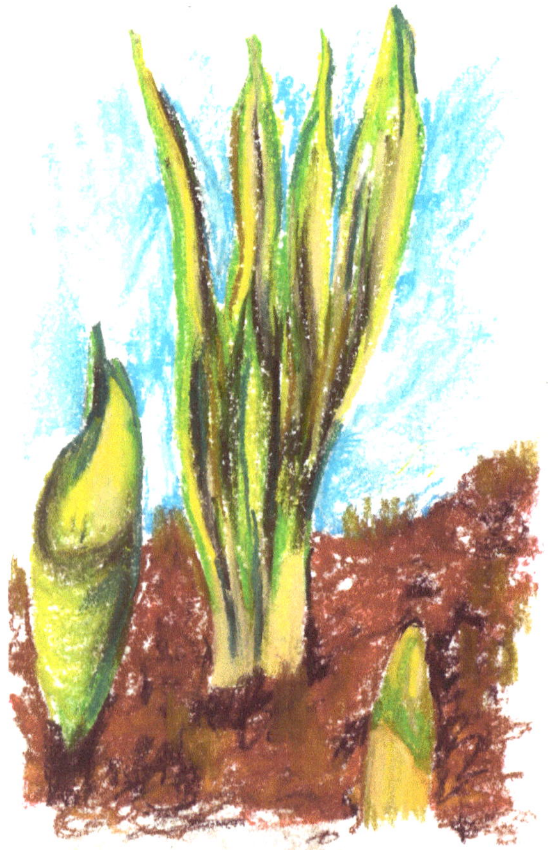

bouncing out of the house, heading toward the car idling at the curb.

There was always more than enough compost for Cecelia's purposes. We usually shared the leftover wheelbarrows full with our neighbors. We lived in a neighborhood where families knew one another. They watched out for one another and shared casseroles. Older kids babysat neighbor's little ones. There were Avon and Tupperware sales, outrageous Halloweens and summer pool parties. What good was a driveway mound of dirt, if it wasn't shared with friends?

A friendly garden competition, amongst the neighboring ladies, endured for years. It was good-natured competition rooted in fun, no envy in our neighborhood.

Each garden was different. Each reflected their owner's personality and yielded a wide variety of planted shapes and colors.

Roy shoveled compost into a neighbor's wheelbarrow. The black dirt was pushed across the street or along the sidewalk winding up in the neighbor garden. None of the stinking black gold was wasted.

Cecelia's attention to planning and detail, in hindsight, was incredible. It revealed a vital aspect of her seasonal vision for flowers and foliage. Yet, she didn't write down her plan or keep a gardening journal. We can only recall her actions, resources, and care that resulted her personal inner *beauty*, exhibited as Cecelia's Garden.

Cecelia's Creative Counsel:

What is your vision?

Do you have a plan?

Cultivate resources and an action plan early in your process. Envision the potential to yield dramatic results, later on.

Don't discount the use of "old school" methods that add simplicity to your process.

Sharing your vision and plan as you enlist your team. Giving each team participant a task that contributes to the end result.

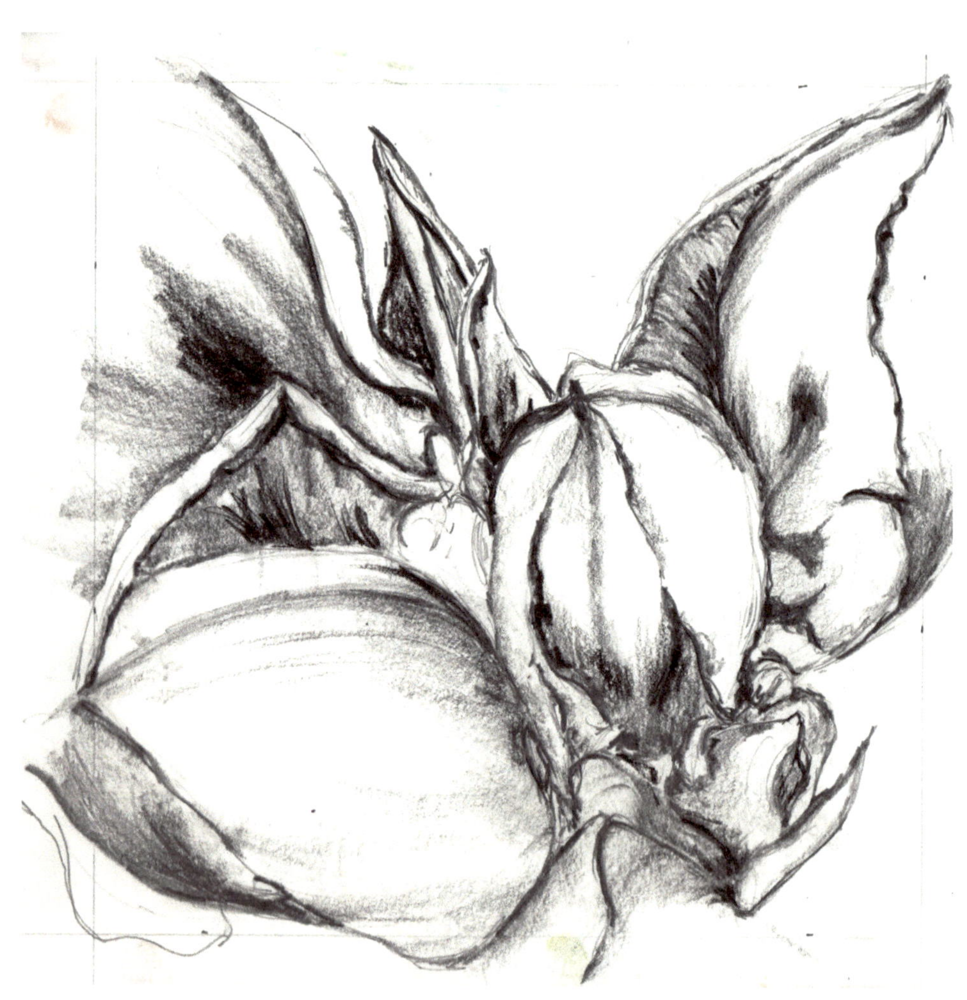

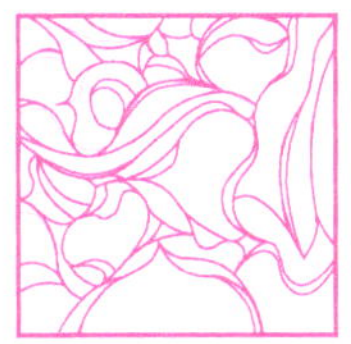

SWEET PEA
ON CHAIN LINK

Every gardener has one little patch somewhere that is unusable, unresponsive ground. Cecelia's dead zone was the northeast corner of the backyard. It had become a wasteland following the installation of the above ground pool. *Where would all the dirt go that became the "deep end"?*

It had always been the "compost corner". Nothing grew there, except weeds. Over time, pulled weeds, trimmed branches, dead headed blooms, failed plants, and grass clippings rotted into compost. Growing larger, yet out-of-sight behind the pool and an evergreen, the pile grew.

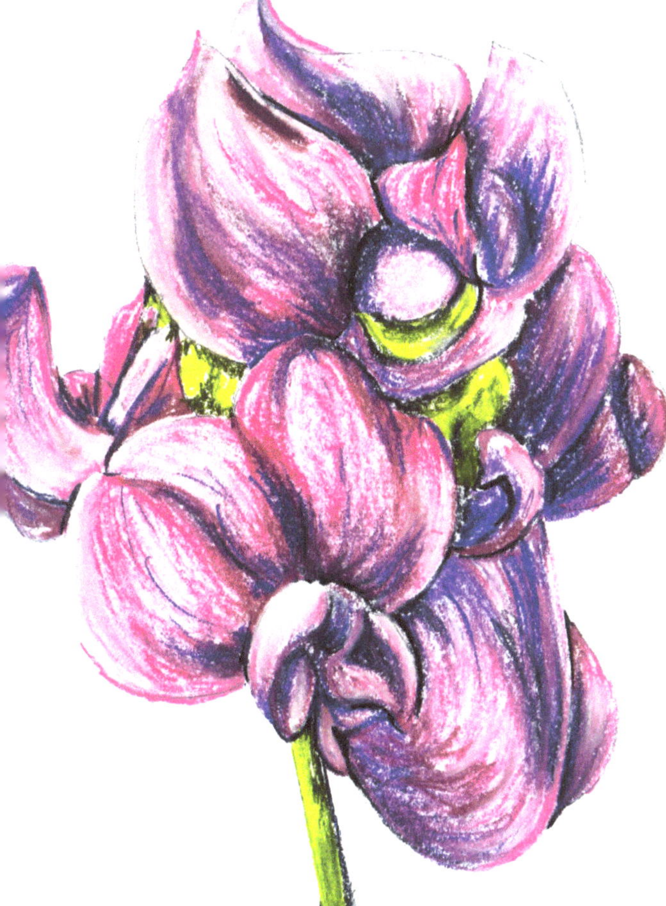

Our neighbor's solution for this unsightly corner was climbing sweet pea and snapdragons. These grew along his section of the fence and became a bright spot.

The openness of the chain link fence was a metaphor for the relationship with [some] neighbors. Cecelia and our next-door neighbor, Jesse, chatted often, regardless of any fence separating the yards.

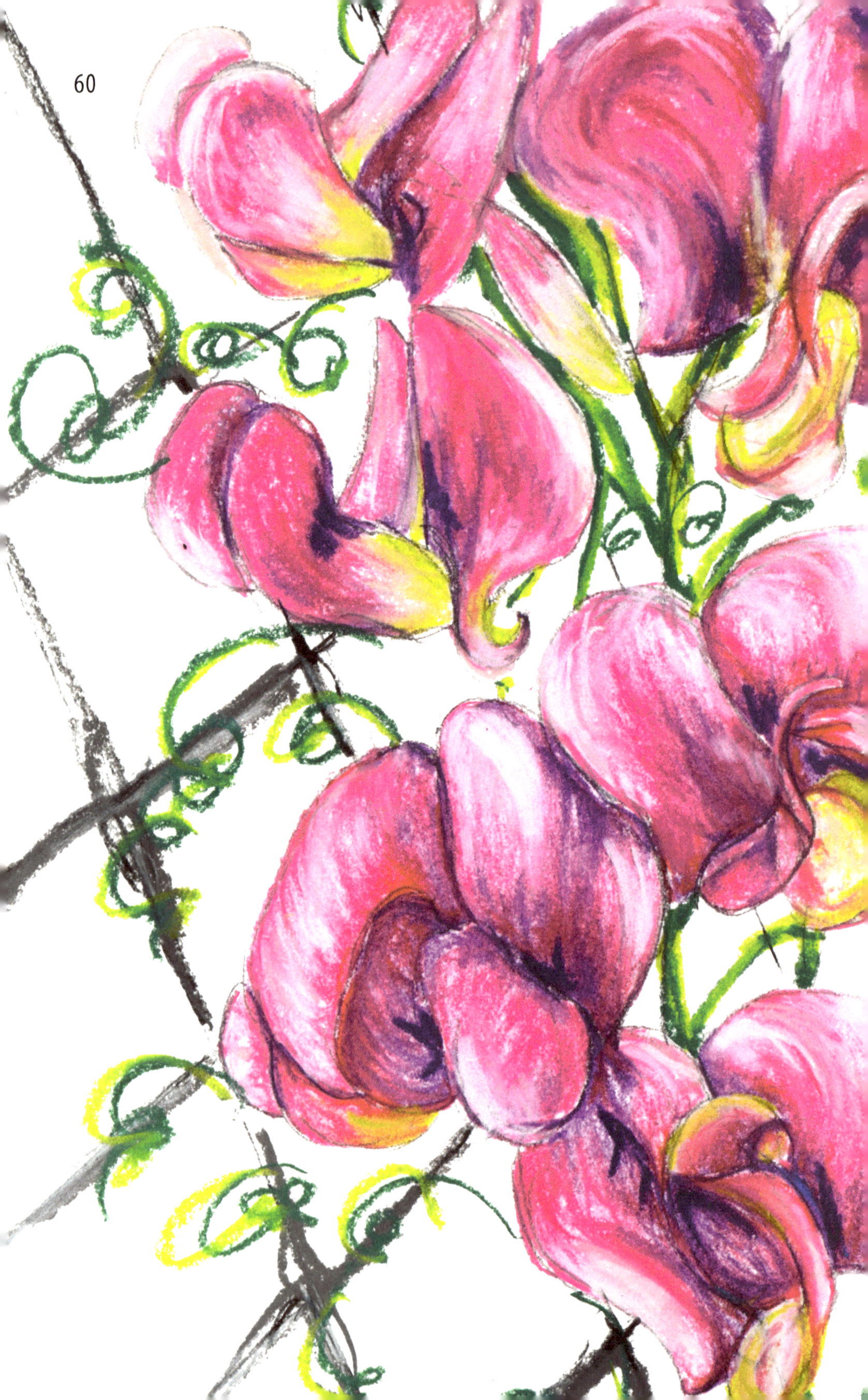

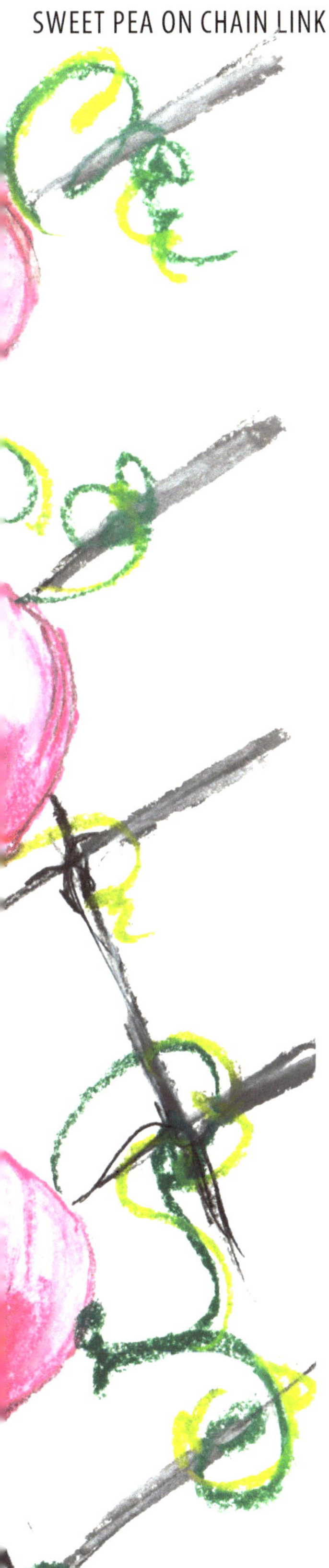

Conversations over coffee or iced tea, a sweet treat; talking neighborhood 'gossip', school news, and family activities.

How does one disguise an ugly chain-link fence? Cecelia did it with shrubs, lilacs, peonies, and honeysuckle. Jesse planted climbing sweet pea and snapdragons, adding color to the barren corner of the shared fencing.

Jesse had her own gardening style. It was an easy-to-care approach using annuals and perennials like hostas, day lilies and her seasonal favorite: begonias.

Another plant she liked was sweet pea. They had their own special sweet fragrance and upward growth pattern. The sweet pea grew up the fence with the vines anchored to the fence by frail curling tendrils. The burst of red, purple, pink, and white tiny blooms were like viewing an Impressionist painting. The gentle fragrance of the sweet pea filled the late spring air, competing with many of the other aromas in the neighborhood.

This was a wise choice for that corner of the yard.

When the sweet pea flowers faded with the heat of summer the climbing vine and the little curly anchors remained. An ideal background for the snapdragons Jesse planted.

Snapdragons can be sowed from seed during the late winter and planted at the break of Spring. They blossomed from the bottom of the stalk upward, similar to a gladiolus. This corner of her garden remained colorful through the end of summer with the addition of snapdragons.

Cecelia's Creative Counsel:

Accept failure as part of the process. Not everything will work out successfully or as expected.

Fail.

Twyla Tharp* describes six types of failure and importance of acceptance and correction.

- Failure of SKILL.
- Failure of CONCEPT.
- Failure of JUDGMENT
- Failure of NERVE.
- Failure of REPETITION.
- Failure from DENIAL.

* The Creative Habit, Learn It and Use It for Life (Simon & Schuster, 2006)

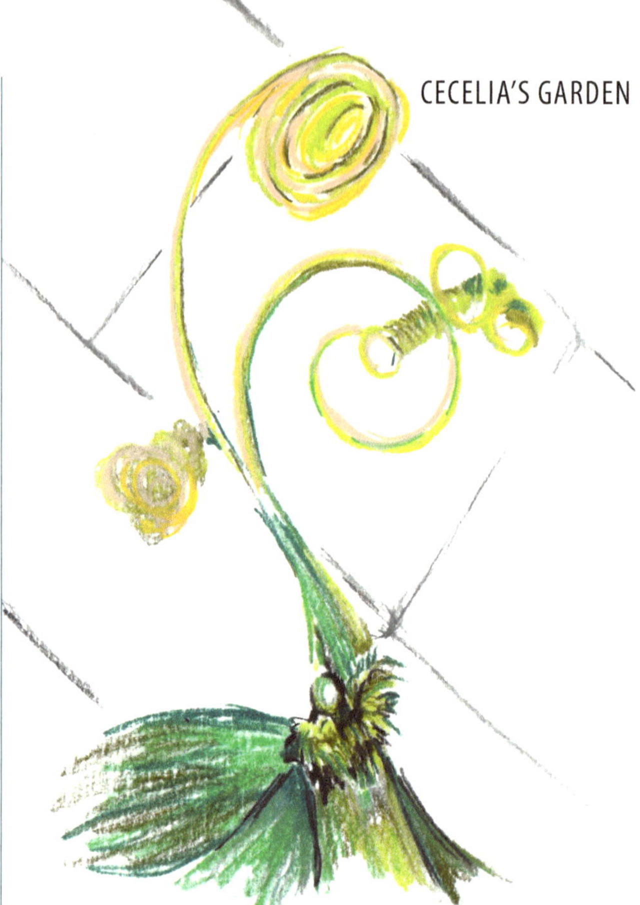

The bright blooms attracting vital pollinators like butterflies, dragonflies, bees and, even, wasps.

These flowers were a hardy choice opposite the abandoned corner of the Cecelia's backyard. The snapdragons were placed side by side, separated by a wire mesh of galvanized steel wire, shielding our year-round compost pile.

Cecelia caught a glimpse of Jesse's sweet pea on the fence as she floated on a pool lounger, sipping her iced tea (or gin & tonic). Cecelia admired the beauty of nature, her distinct Duchene smile light up her face, in appreciation of Jesse's success; another positive neighborhood link.

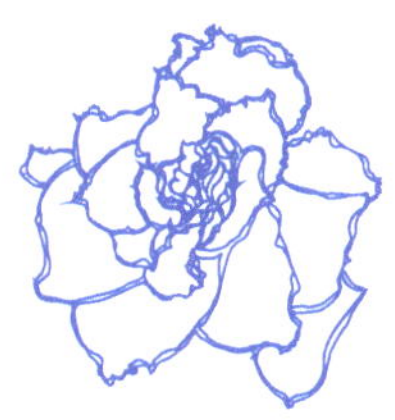

PLUSH PEONIES

Cecelia's peonies were show stoppers!

In full bloom, the blossoms were soft and fluffy, like cotton balls. Their gentle pastel colors whispered femininity, and were yet another reflection of the gardener.

Recalling the overall layout of Cecelia's Garden and the location of plants with its color schematic bring back a memory that could have been created by a professional garden layout artist. Cecelia's back yard gardens began with her roses. Their characteristic rich dark red and orange hues gradually became the pastel tones of the peonies that further transitioned into her keystone honeysuckle. Everything nested in the corner, separating the peonies from the roses.

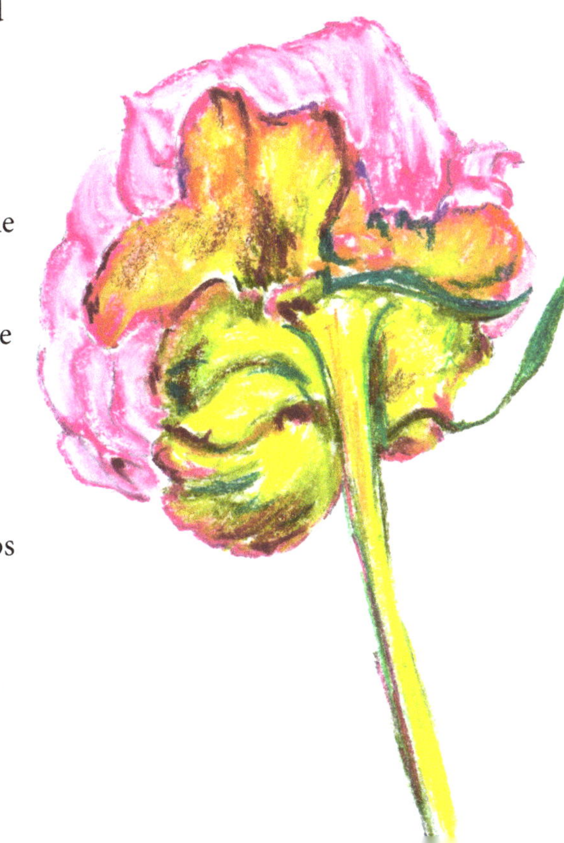

Planted along the north side of the backyard, the peonies were bathed in light from morning to afternoon. They were in an ideal location for the "paenoia" to flourish.

Cecelia devoted much attention and care to her peonies. They were, like her roses, an investment in of years of nurturing. The young shrubs had grown to maturity.

Instead of purchasing a potted peony shrub for cultivation, Cecelia opted for bare-root plant. It started out as a small plant. No fuss digging a deep hole; Cecelia added compost with her "secret" natural additive. There was some kind of protectorate to safeguard against invasive rodents, insects and disease that can harm, even destroy, a peony.

To aid the peony's growth, Cecelia inserted stakes and/or a wire frame for sturdiness. Continued maintenance, feeding and inspecting the buds; searching out insects and fungi also helped her plants flourish. In the autumn, Cecelia asked Roy to cut the stalks back to ground level and place a blanket of straw over the garden for winter.

Season-after-season maintenance.

It began with nothing, but dirt.

By the time Cecelia's garden reached maturity, she had a collection of six to eight healthy, blooming peony shrubs. Under a master gardener's care, peonies can produce blooms for fifty or more years. A masterful gardener, Cecelia tended this garden for about thirty years.

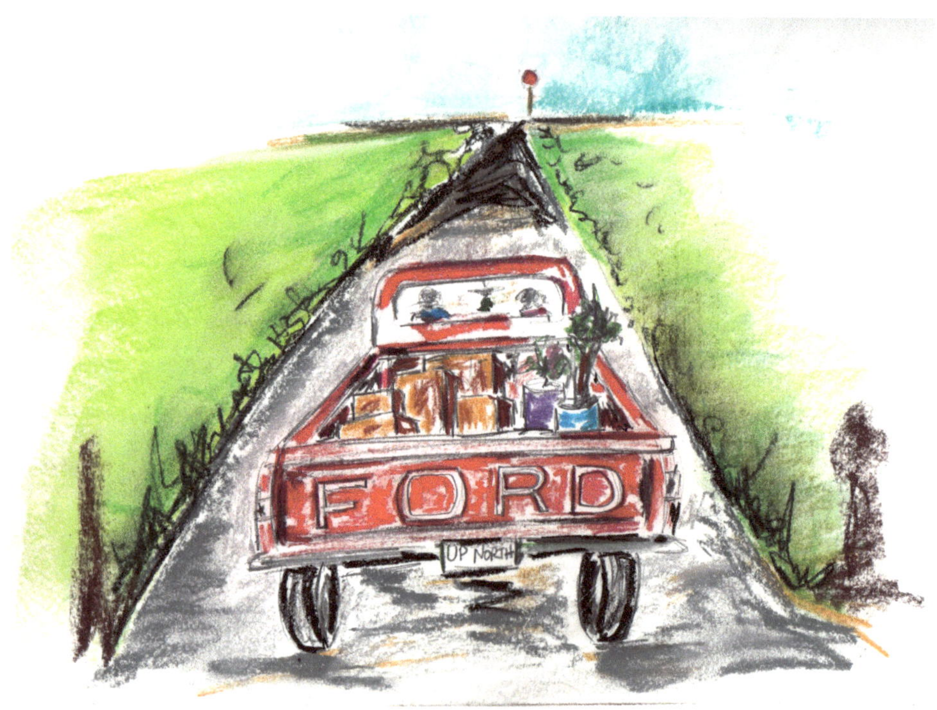

The peony is a favorite, sought after year around and a top choice for brides. However, its blooming cycle is very short, not to be missed.

Pat, her fiery redhead daughter, was enchanted with the peonies, Pat believed that they were a symbol of grace and luxury. She assisted Mom and learned Cecelia's techniques. It turned out to be an investment that paid out in spades, when Pat transplanted several shrubs to her own garden.

The peonies continued to prosper at Pat's new lake house garden.

Eventually Roy and Cecelia fell in love with the "Up North" lifestyle. They decided to become transplants from the suburbs. A 'FOR SALE' sign was posted and the process of downsizing began. Anxious for a change from their suburban house, a place they called home for nearly thirty years, Roy and Cecelia moved.

The peonies would become part of a new garden where Cecelia could still participate in the seasonal process, somewhat.

Everything about the peony, except for the buds, is symbolic of fragility, from the framework for growth to the petals of the flowers. The open peony reveals its simple structure, the outer petals surrounding the pollen-bearing anthers that surround the pistil.

You can also look for the ants!

Cecelia's Creative Counsel:

Share your talent and skills with others.

Pass along your 'gift' of experience and knowledge, step into the role of the teacher. Let someone be your apprentice.

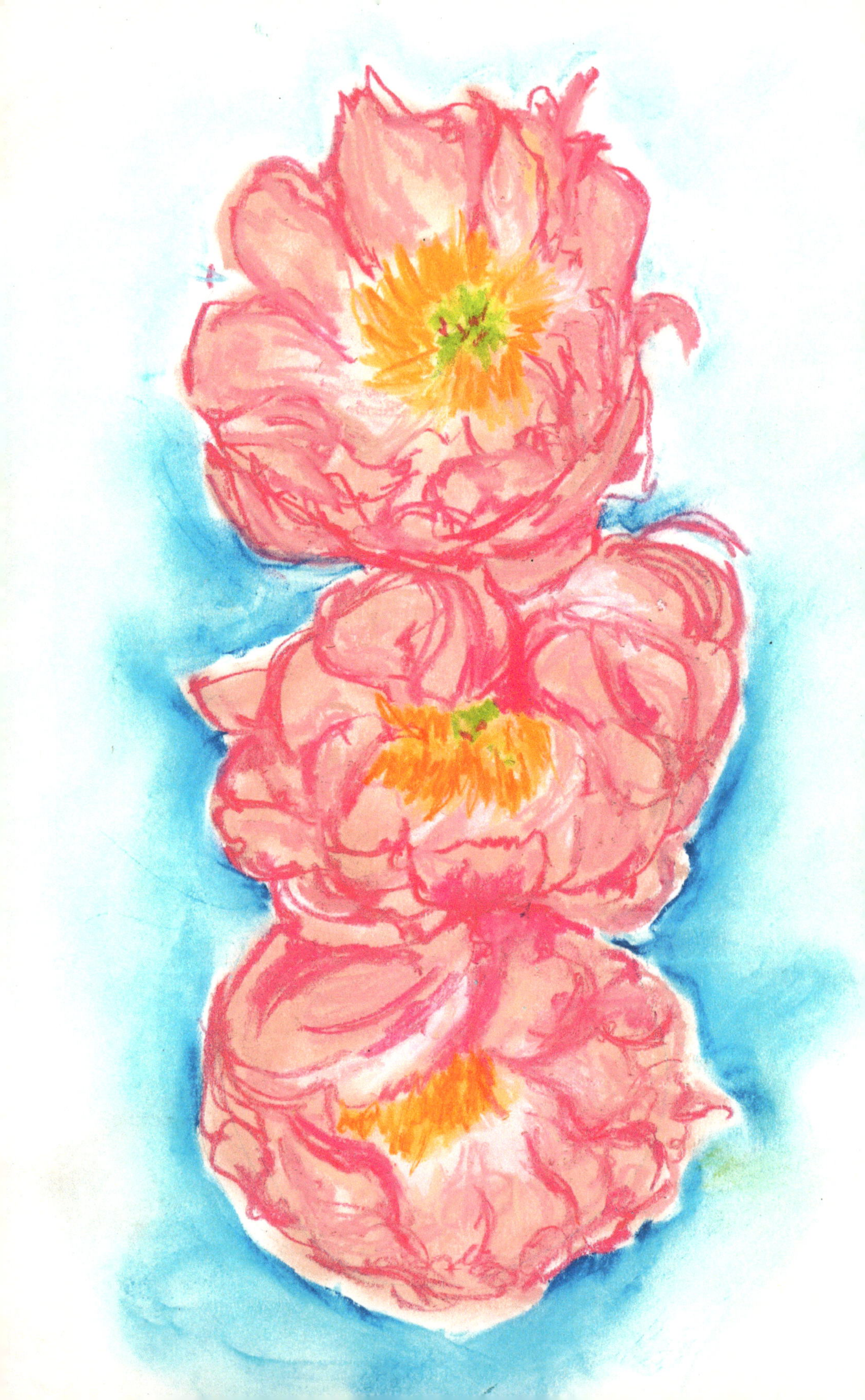

FIVE TYPES OF CREATIVE THINKING

"The plants have enough spirit to transform our limited vision."
— Rosemary Gladstar

1. Convergent: Crazy curiosity of exploring more than one idea or thought to form a new or different entity. Experiment with how the unrelated fit together; i.e. lion + tiger = liger.

2. Divergent: aka Reverse Engineering. Disassemble. Take it apart. Examine the individual pieces. Find a common factor.

   Are there any relationships between the parts?

3. Lateral: Logical thinking in a straight line. Seeking a solution to a problem via traditional (orthodox) methods. Looks for new ways.

4. Aesthetic: Focusing on 'how' an object looks. The visual and spatial attributes. Structure, composition, color, shape, patterns. Other senses, smell and taste can be a factor.

5. Emergent: Deep thinking. A natural process is the result from rumination, meditation, daydreaming, walking, journaling. {Can} Result in "AHA" moment.

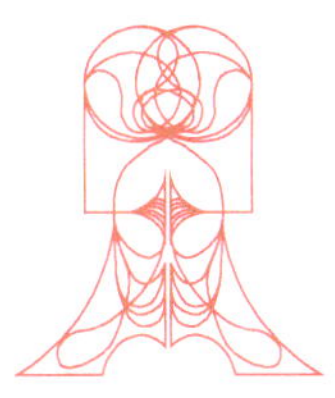

CONCLUSION

Writing and illustrating this book has been a 'labor of love', painstaking and joyous at the same time. It all started with a memory, a flashback that hit me unexpectedly.

The impetus for most of the stories were triggered by the part-time job I have/had at the Floral Dept of my local grocery store. Every week boxes of flowers coming in and going out. Helping customers select flowers for gift giving occasions like birthdays, promotions, get well, congratulations, sympathy and "get me out of the dog house."

The "Wet Wrap" story was the beginning of this humble book. Writing, long-hand, the memory and jotting down the visuals of our childhood home. The vision came to me when I was preparing a bouquet of lilacs for a customer. He asked how to keep the stems fresh for the drive out to suburbia. The 'aha' moment was the connection with lilacs and the wet wrap technique.

Little things that stir the memory and hit you unexpectedly... *serendipity.*

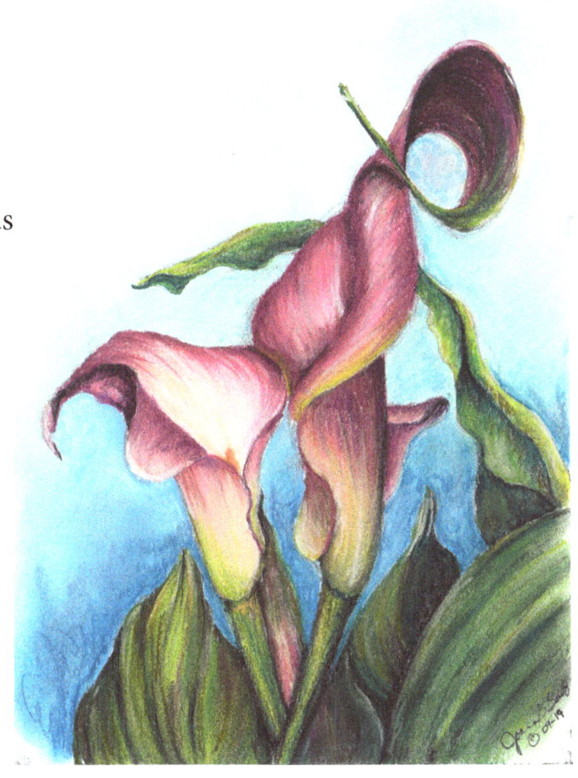

ABOUT JOANN

Just a woman, raised in suburban Detroit, attended public school and put myself through college. Moved to Chicago when I was twenty one, moved back to Michigan a couple times... eventually moving back to Chicago.

My own family is VERY creative. Dominic, my spouse is a photographer and writer. Our daughter, Geena, is applying the creative problem solving lessons we used in our parenting. Our youngest daughter, Amanda, is about to graduate from college and begin her own creative career, she's been applying creative thinking to projects and daily life.

I'm ready to plan the next phase of my life continuing to learn about creative thinking the importance it has on us.

The lilacs were just the beginning, more memories blossomed; some more easily than others.

The hyacinths and tulips arriving in the store prompted the vision of Mom's bulb garden. Following some research about bulb care and gardening, I began to realize that Cecelia was a true gardener.

Lugging the forty-pound boxes of gladiolus, which our store received week-after-week in the spring, took me deeper into my childhood. Recalling more details about the individual gardens, the old baby dresser reused as her 'she shed', local retailers, and my family.

Another pattern began to emerge within each of the stories, the influence my mother, Cecelia, had on me (and my siblings) as a creative mentor.

I truly believe she was unaware of the impact she had on our ability to apply creative problem solving to everyday situations. Granted, our father also played a major role, as well. (*More about that in my next book.*) Together, the lessons they taught us have been indispensable.

I've spent my life investing in a creative career, studying art, creative thinking and pursuing projects and opportunities to advance my skills and utilize my talents as a designer, artist and speaker.

Cecelia's Garden is the allegory to illustrate how EVERYONE can use creative thinking and problem solving EVERYDAY.

www.ingramcontent.com/pod-product-compliance
Lightning Source LLC
LaVergne TN
LVHW052257100826
845147LV00001B/69

9780984895076